"Have dinner night."

"What—like a date?" Natalia asked.

"Yes, a date," Giancarlo confirmed. "One where we get to know each other outside the work environment...." He touched her soft, crushable lip with a finger.

She knew what he was saying—the sultry look in her deceitful eyes told him so, as did the sensual pulse in the air surrounding them. And as his body throbbed, and his anger roared, and his eyes burned with his intentions, he felt those soft lips move on her answer.

"Yes," she said.

Triumph sang in his blood. She was his for the taking, and he *was* going to take her. By the time this thing was over, Natalia Deyton was going to belong to *him* body and soul, Giancarlo vowed.

Body and wretched, lying soul....

Michelle Reid

A SICILIAN SEDUCTION

RED HOT REVENGE

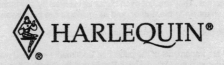

HARLEQUIN®

TORONTO • NEW YORK • LONDON
AMSTERDAM • PARIS • SYDNEY • HAMBURG
STOCKHOLM • ATHENS • TOKYO • MILAN • MADRID
PRAGUE • WARSAW • BUDAPEST • AUCKLAND

ISBN 0-373-12175-X

A SICILIAN SEDUCTION

First North American Publication 2001.

CHAPTER ONE

GIANCARLO CARDINALE arrived in the doorway of Knight's executive dining room to the surprise discovery that some kind of function was taking place. The remains of a gourmet-style lunch still lay in evidence amongst a scatter of empty wine bottles, and the twenty or so people who were gathered there were now standing around in small groups talking while they sipped at champagne.

'What's going on?' he asked the man beside him.

'Lunch between presentations to one of our best clients,' Howard Fiske explained. 'And Edward really should have made the effort to be here for it.'

His anger was clear. If it wasn't bad enough that the corporate chairman himself should have turned up here unexpectedly, to have done so on a day when Edward should have been presiding over such an important meeting, annoyed Howard intensely.

Giancarlo said nothing, but he sympathised. He knew all about Edward's irresponsible streak, after all. In fact Edward's flagrant lack of responsibility on all fronts was the sole reason for his being in London. He had come to deal with it once and for all, and the sooner he got it over with the better it was going to be for everyone. Which left him with only one question he needed answering before he got down to the nasty business of dealing with the problem.

Which one was she?

As he stood there, still unnoticed by the rest of the gathering, his gaze began moving over the newly refurbished ultra-modern room with its beech-wood surfaces and flashes of so-called inspirational colour—all paid for with his money in an attempt to haul Knight's out of the dark ages.

But it was not so easy to revamp the people, he observed, seeing the same starched collars and the same grey faces, with their grey little minds which collectively helped to keep the company in a state of near peril.

His teeth came together on a snap of irritation. Edward had promised to restructure his workforce last year when they'd discussed merging Knight's into the Cardinale Group. In fact, Giancarlo had insisted upon it before he would agree to ratify the deal. Edward might be his brother-in-law but the Cardinale Group was not run as a charity. As a venture capitalist Giancarlo looked for potential in any proposed merger before he even considered putting together a rescue package.

Edward had been told this, had understood it, and had agreed to all the provisos at the time. So—other than for laminate flooring and some splashes of colour on the walls—where had all the money he had been steadily shelling out to Edward gone? For none of these grey, slightly bored faces he could see in here showed a hint of a change in attitude.

Which was why Giancarlo had no problem at all picking out his quarry, since she was the only one that fitted the description his source had provided him with, of a young, very nubile, bottle redhead, with an inherent ability to distract any man.

If this really was Natalia Deyton, then Edward could certainly pick them, Giancarlo decided as he stood watching the way she worked around the room like a true professional.

Professional in what? he then found himself pondering

cynically as his darkly lashed gaze shifted from her admittedly exquisite profile to the revealingly flushed one belonging to the young man she was talking to at present. Her job description had her down as the personal assistant to Knight's namesake and managing director. But with a face and a figure like that, it wasn't surprising that Edward Knight had given her job title a whole new twist.

Anger suddenly began to bite as he stood watching the provocative way she was teasing that blushing young fool. Tying him in knots, he saw. Making it plain that she was open to suggestion.

Brazen bitch, he thought sourly. Then—

Brazen *bountiful* bitch, he found himself extending when the crowd suddenly shifted and he got a glimpse of what it was that was hooking their attention. She had the kind of cleavage a man could dive into—as her skimpy white top with its dipping neckline was blatantly advertising!

No wonder half the men in here looked hot about their starched collars. And no wonder Edward couldn't keep his damn hands off her, Giancarlo added harshly when he felt even his own more discerning loins give him a stinging kick that actually forced him to draw the muscles in around his sex to stop the obvious from happening.

'*Dio,*' he breathed, when as if sensing his scrutiny she suddenly turned to look straight at him.

Those eyes, those amazing eyes! He had never encountered anything like them! Blue, they were blue. A smoky, steamy, sultry blue that had his imagination shooting into overdrive as he began to wonder what happened to those eyes when she was beneath a man and in the throes of an orgasm.

Did Edward already know? Was he still man enough to acquire that heady kind of knowledge? Giancarlo's sister said no. In fact his sister had been quite disconcertingly open about Edward's recent inability to satisfy her on that front. But this was different. The woman standing here could incite a dying man to take one last sip of the nectar.

Without any warning, a new kind of emotion was suddenly overwhelming him. It was a hot, tight, primitive emotion that sank its roots deep into his possessive psyche, where it lashed him with the burning message that he did not *want* Edward to know what Natalia Deyton was like in bed. He didn't want any other man but *himself* to know what, in that single blinding hot flash of a moment, he knew he fully intended to make his exclusively…!

Oh, good grief! Natalia found herself gasping inwardly as she caught the full heat of the stranger's expression. In all her life she had never encountered a look quite like it. Men looked at her and wanted her, she was used to that. She would be lying if she tried to deny an effect she had been having on the opposite sex for most of her adult life.

But the way this man was looking at her was something else entirely. It was hot and compulsive and so very possessive that she actually felt as if he were crawling right inside her skin and claiming total occupancy.

Stunned and shaken by the whole experience, she quickly dragged her eyes away. But too late to stop a tight, breathlessly excited feeling from permeating her blood, and, although she tried very hard to concentrate on the conversation taking place around her, she was really hearing nothing but a strange roaring taking place in her head. Her eyes had glazed over, leaving only a mirror image imprinted on her retina of a tall, lean, very attractive stranger with black hair, olive skin and dark, dark compelling eyes that even now, while she wasn't actually looking into them, still made her feel as if she were being invaded. Who was he? What was he? Why was he standing there looking at her like that?

It was almost impossible not to look back at him—just to check that he was real and the small sip of champagne she had allowed herself hadn't started her hallucinating.

It was most definitely a relief to find Howard Fiske had claimed his attention. But the power of the physical man still seriously disturbed her. Everything—everything about him from the long, slightly hooked shape of his nose that should have spoilt his playboy good looks but didn't, to the lean tight structure of his body clothed in the finest Italian tailoring, affirmed the man's sexual appeal. He oozed it, pulsed it, threatened and promised it.

Oh, my God—she looked away again, so appalled by her own lustful thoughts that they made the sexual way he had been looking at her fade into insignificance.

'Are you feeling all right, Natalia?' a voice from what seemed like a long distance off managed to squeeze its way into her consciousness.

'Yes,' she replied, though it took all she had in her to find the light, reassuring smile to go with the answer. 'But I think the champagne is beginning to get to me.' Another passable smile—a rueful one—and she placed her glass down on the nearest table. 'Never could take alcohol during daylight. Another sip and I would probably end up snoring for the rest of the day.'

'You would never snore...' Very intense, deadly serious—it was almost a relief to look into Ian Gant's besotted eyes because his boyish attraction to her was so easy to deal with.

'Tell me about your lovely fiancée,' she urged, glancing briefly to his left as she did so. 'The wedding is only a few weeks away, I believe?'

It was enough. He took the hint. The flush of attraction

changed to a flush of embarrassment when he recalled the presence of Randall Taylor, his future father-in-law who, hearing weddings mentioned, turned to join in the discussion.

After that she was able to put the stranger out of her mind while she concentrated on the business in hand. Which was, in part, supposed to be an exercise in public relations because Taylor-Gant were threatening to take their business elsewhere if Knight's did not improve their overall performance.

A grave step—a tough step when you took into consideration that Taylor-Gant had been using Edward's marketing skills since for ever.

The sudden tap on her shoulder had her turning with a smile at the ready for whomever it was who wanted her attention.

But the smile died the moment she found herself looking down at Howard Fiske. Cold-eyed, mean-mouthed, and with the naturally aggressive manner that seemed to come along with his short, thin stature, he drew her apart from the others with a set of fingers on her arm that dug in just a little too tightly for her liking.

'Your presence is required,' he said, flicking his eyes to her cleavage with an insolence that made her grit her teeth. 'Edward's office. As of now.'

Edward—the magic word. 'He's turned up at last?' she exclaimed, so relieved she couldn't contain it. But she had been worrying about him throughout the whole morning when it had become clear that he'd gone missing without telling anyone. It wasn't the first time he'd done this recently, but this particular day it had been important that he be here to soothe the Taylor-Gant ruffled feathers. But Edward wasn't thinking too clearly at the moment, due to a struggle he was having with himself. *Many* struggles, she then extended painfully. To him his whole life was in a mess and he just didn't know what to do to make it better.

'Just excuse yourself and go,' Howard Fiske tersely instructed. And as he removed his fingers from her arm she was almost positive they brushed against the side of her breast quite deliberately.

It made her want to shudder, though she contained the need, having learned very early on in her six-month conflict with Howard Fiske that a response—any kind of response to his blatant touching—was just what gave the nasty man his kicks.

So with a blank face she nodded in silent acquiescence, then turned to make her excuses.

'That girl is a credit to this company,' Randall Taylor remarked as he, too, watched the way she took her leave of each person in turn before eventually escaping through the door.

You wouldn't be saying that if she were bedding your future son-in-law behind your daughter's back, Howard thought with a smile that hid his real contempt for Edward's so-called *personal* assistant as he watched her slip quietly out of the room.

Suddenly he felt almost happy, because he had a very good feeling that Natalia Deyton was about to meet her Waterloo—or Giancarlo Cardinale was not the man he was reputed to be...

Natalia, on the other hand, was too busy worrying about Edward to think about anything else as she took the direct route across the dove-grey carpet covering her own office floor on her way to Edward's office.

The door was firmly shut, but it didn't deter her. With only a cursory knock to warn of her arrival, she opened it and sailed right in there with all guns blazing. 'Edward—you have to know that I am very angry with you,' she announced. 'I really can't believe that you've let everyone down like this! Where have you been all morning? What is it you—'

'It's not Edward,' a smooth, deep, totally unfamiliar voice with the merest thread of a foreign accent inserted.

In the process of closing the door behind her, Natalia spun on her slender heels then froze, totally stunned to see the tall dark stranger from the dining room comfortably ensconced in the chair behind Edward's desk, and looking as if he had every right to be there!

He had even removed the jacket to his dark suit, so the bright white of his shirt stood out against the black leather back of Edward's chair, adding extra emphasis to the width of his shoulders and the breadth of his chest, which set that same tight, tense breathless feeling that had attacked her earlier stinging through her system.

It was awful—stifling and confusing because she didn't understand what was happening here! Not the tingling sensation, nor the baffling fact that some total stranger seemed to have taken up residence in Edward's office. And what was just as bad was the way he was running those eyes over her again as if he had every right to do that also!

'Who are you?' she demanded. 'What right have you to be in here?'

He didn't even bother to answer. Instead he just continued to inspect her from the top of her gleaming head to the tips of her shiny black leather court shoes. It was like being stripped to the bare skin by a pair of black lasers, she likened, automatically stiffening up in outright objection.

'I asked you a question,' she snapped out.

'Actually, you asked two,' he drawled in a soft, dry,

husky tone that had her stomach muscles curling in on themselves in response.

A sensual response, she noted in helpless confusion. What was wrong with her? Who was he, and why was he making her feel like this?

It was deliberate too; she was at least functioning sharply enough to be aware of the hint of calculation behind his lazily seductive regard.

'I'm going to call Security,' she announced, turning back to the door again.

'Three questions, if we include the one you thought you were asking Edward,' he tagged on very silkily.

And like a trigger that had the power to control her every movement, his use of Edward's name had her freezing yet again as a few very salient points began to filter into her stunned brain cells at last.

She'd first seen him standing with Howard. Now he was installed behind Edward's desk. And he had removed his suit jacket, which suggested that he intended to be there for quite some time. The jacket to his *Italian*-made suit, which went so well with his rich, dark *Italian* accent.

Oh, no. Her heart sank as full understanding finally hit her, and her skin began to prickle for a completely different reason. 'Giancarlo Cardinale,' she breathed out unsteadily.

'Well done,' he commended with a smile she didn't like. 'Now, please...' he waved a hand towards the chair opposite him '...come and sit down, Miss Deyton. We need to talk, I think, and we may as well be comfortable while we do so.'

But now she'd had his identity confirmed, she had no wish to move another inch away from this door until she had a few important answers. 'What's happened to

Edward?' she asked in a short, tense voice that revealed her anxiety. 'Is he all right? Has he taken ill?'

Anger leapt to life so abruptly in those lazy dark eyes that it took her completely aback. 'Nothing has happened to Edward,' he clipped out. 'Edward is *never* ill—as I am sure you are already aware of.'

Natalia didn't like his tone. It stiffened her backbone, as did the cold cynicism suddenly hardening his expression.

So what had happened to bring about a change in his attitude? And where *was* Edward? It was a question that sent a sudden cold little chill chasing down her spine. 'His wife, then,' she prompted, too anxious to realise that she was treading a very unstable line here. 'Has your sister taken ill or something?'

From anger, Giancarlo Cardinale turned to ice. 'You ask a lot of questions for a lowly clerk,' he incised.

'I am not a lowly clerk,' she denied.

'What are you, then?'

If it was possible her backbone went even straighter— and seemed to become a live conduit for the warning shot of electricity that went tingling down its full length. He couldn't know, could he? Warily she studied his dark face for any clues as to what exactly was going on because something dire certainly was, or he wouldn't be here like this.

Had he found out about her relationship with Edward…?

Sitting there watching the play of emotions taking place on her face, Giancarlo was experiencing a quiet sense of satisfaction for having so quickly brought her to the point where she was considering the frightening prospect of full exposure.

And who would not be frightened in similar circumstances? he allowed. If she had managed to work that much out, then she had also remembered that the blood that ran in his veins was Sicilian, and to a Sicilian family honour meant everything, which meant that she was in deep trouble.

Yet—oddly—he didn't want her afraid of him, though barely an hour ago he had been walking into this building looking forward to frightening the life out of Natalia Deyton—before he kicked her out of here.

Now things had changed. His game plan had changed. He had looked into her eyes and seen a sensual heaven beckoning him that he could not ignore. He wanted to experience that heaven. He wanted to touch it, taste it, lose himself in it. He wanted to spend days and nights and long exquisite weeks exploring all its possibilities to the exclusion of none—before he kicked her out.

Which also meant that he needed her to see him as her hero not as her enemy if he was going to convince her to let *him* in her bed instead of Edward.

Not that Giancarlo doubted for a second that this was exactly what she was going to do, because, no matter how beautiful she was to look at, he had not forgotten that a cold and calculatingly mercenary woman lurked beneath all of that beauty. Why else would she choose a paunchy middle-aged man like Edward for her lover if it weren't out of avarice?

Or was money her big turn-on? he then wondered cynically. Well, if it was, he decided, then he possessed more of that spicy commodity than Edward could ever hope to offer. Nor was he middle-aged or paunchy...

But his time was limited. He had put six weeks aside in his busy work schedule to be here in London. Six weeks to woo her, thoroughly slake his lusts in her—then redress family honour in a way that Natalia Deyton would never forget in a lifetime.

Still, first came the sweetness before the vengeance, he told himself, recognising the tight sting of anticipation for exactly what it was as he prepared to make her fall on him in undying gratitude.

'My apologies, Miss Deyton,' he murmured suddenly. 'I have clearly upset you, and I had no wish to do that. Please, come and sit down, and I will explain to you why I am here.'

She blinked and went pale but began moving towards him. Watching her do so was a pleasure in itself. The graceful stretch of her legs, the sway of her hips, and the unbelievable amount of sensuality she displayed from slender shoulders to beautiful feet. Even the way she lowered herself into the chair on the other side of the desk possessed a kind of poetry. And her hair was not bottle red but a natural burnished copper that caught fire in the weak sunlight seeping into the room from behind him, enhancing her amazing milk-white skin.

He missed none of it—wanted all of it. Especially that mouth, he decided. That soft, gorgeous mouth which was already parted and trembling slightly as if inviting him in.

But the eyes were no longer looking sultry. They looked scared. He wanted sultry. To get it, he leaned forward in the chair, using sexual body language to grab her attention. It worked; her lashes flickered slightly as her gaze dropped from his face to his shirtfront as it came closer. The hairs covering his chest began to prickle in indication of his own sexual arousal.

The spice of life, he named it dryly, noting the way her breathing quickened and her breasts lifted and fell beneath the fitted white top, as her own indication of sexual arousal. Deciding to consolidate on that, he got up and walked round to settle his lean hips on the desk only a few short inches away from her.

'Edward is well,' he assured her, watching the way her eyes slid down the length of his legs—then quickly away again. 'My sister Alegra is also well,' he added. 'In fact they are at this moment enjoying a well-deserved holiday cruising the Caribbean.'

Surprise brought her eyes up to clash with his. 'But— Edward never said—'

'Because Edward didn't know anything about it.' Giancarlo smiled. 'The cruise was arranged as a surprise present from me for their silver wedding anniversary,' he explained. 'You did know that Edward and my sister have been married for twenty-five years?' he then slid in silkily.

She shifted uncomfortably. 'Yes,' she confirmed.

Yes, he repeated silently. Of course you know. This was supposed to be the point where he duly informed her of what *he* knew about her affair with Edward—before he told her to get the hell out of his brother-in-law's life while she still had a chance to do it in one piece. He even had the fat cheque already made out and waiting in his pocket, to give a little impetus to her departure.

But the cheque remained where it was, and he no longer wanted Natalia Deyton to escape in one piece. He wanted to retain certain parts of her, the secrets of her beautiful body for one, the key to her heart for another.

Vengeance, sweet vengeance, he named it poetically. The Sicilian in him had no difficulty at all squaring his intentions with his conscience.

'The trip was planned in complete secrecy, and dropped on them both without warning a mere hour before they had to leave for Heathrow airport,' he expounded with a wry look that acknowledged the necessity to give neither of them the time to think about it. 'The surprise also came with my personal assurance to Edward that I would come and take care of things here for him while he is away, so he could have no excuse to protest the speed with which he and Alegra were rushed off to catch a flight to Barbados, from where they will begin their cruise.'

'On one of your cruise-liners?' she asked as a glimmer of understanding began to hit her blue eyes.

They weren't sultry but at least they were no longer frightened. 'What else?' He smiled. 'Honeymoon suite, royal deck, no luxury spared. Your concern for their well-being does you proud, Miss Deyton,' he then said with blatant flattery. 'But my own concern for their well-being would not offer them anything less than the very best to help them get over the tragic year they've had.'

Another magic word, he made grim note as she came jerking to her feet at the mention of the tragedy. Her eyes began changing again, clouding over—though not into the sultry expression he had been aiming for. What he saw was guilt. It showed she possessed a conscience, he supposed, though what that guilt was confirming to him did his resolve no favours.

Maybe he should just revert back to his original plan and throw her out of here! he considered on a sudden rise of black anger that hardened his expression, when he recalled the terrible year his sister had just endured since the violent death of her son—her only child—in a car accident. Marco had been the shining light in Alegra's life. When that light had been snuffed out, the family had feared she would never survive the darkness that had followed.

So to discover her husband had found solace from his grief in a woman half the age of his wife was a sin no self-respecting Sicilian could forgive. As he stood there, staring into Natalia Deyton's pained blue eyes, he had a dreadful urge to reach out and choke the very life out of her!

It therefore came as a complete shock to have her reach out and gently touch his shoulder. 'I'm so sorry for your loss,' she softly murmured. 'Edward told me how close you were to Marco. It must have been a terrible time for all of you.'

She had seen his anger and was mistaking it for pain, Giancarlo realised. And her touch on his shoulder was making the taut flesh beneath it crawl with revulsion.

Liar, he then immediately scoffed at his own interpretation. His flesh was tingling with pleasure, not revulsion. Just as his heart was beginning to beat that bit harder because her eyes were sultry at last! And the idea of reverting back to his original plan suddenly lost its appeal because there was much more satisfaction to be gained from slaking and slaking and slaking himself in this woman—before he tossed her onto the heap she belonged upon.

Though that *heap* at this precise moment had taken on the shape and form of a bed of tumbled linen. He could see her stretched out on it, naked and aware, inviting him with those amazing eyes to take anything he wanted from her.

A much more satisfying form of vengeance, he decided, knowing, even as he told himself that, that he was responding to the weakness of his own burning flesh rather than to the incisive intellect he was much better known for.

It didn't stop him, though, from reaching up to touch a gentle finger to the corner of her beautiful mouth. 'Thank you,' he murmured. 'For your understanding.'

The mouth quivered beneath his touch. Her eyes were growing darker, her cheeks slightly flushed, and he felt himself being drawn slowly downwards until his mouth was within a mere hair's breadth of tasting pure heaven.

Abruptly she jerked away, and with a rather dazed shake of her head took a couple of unsteady steps backwards, almost falling over the chair she had been sitting in, in her haste to put some distance between them.

Giancarlo watched and said nothing, in this case deciding that silence was golden when only a fool would misread the signals passing between them.

Having placed what she seemed to believe was a safe distance between them, Natalia composed herself then—quite bravely, he thought—looked him directly in the eye. 'How long will Edward be away?' she asked.

He almost smiled at that cool little voice, but managed to control the urge. 'Six weeks,' he replied, watching her lovely skin take on that milk-white pallor again as she took in this last piece of shocking information.

She was seeing six weeks of hell ahead of her while she tried to fight her own feelings, he suspected. He gave her a week—at the most. And made no effort whatsoever to hide his own sexual awareness. His eyes remained dark and his expression intense, the message he was conveying so clear that she blushed and had to look away again.

'Edward assured me of your *full co-operation* in his absence,' he informed her dulcetly, ruthlessly piling innuendo on innuendo with all the masculine charm at his Sicilian fingertips. 'And I do not see us having a problem getting on with each other—do you?'

'N-no, of course not,' she agreed with as much professional cool as she could muster. But she was looking quite satisfyingly flustered as she turned her back on him to stare at the door in a rather desperate need for escape now. 'Is—is there anything I can get for you?' she asked as desperation became an uncontrollable desire and she began walking on unsteady legs towards the door.

'Coffee would be nice,' he said. 'Black, preferably Italian if you can lay your hands on any.'

She nodded and kept walking.

'Plus all the files on Edward's major clients,' he added more briskly. 'Specifically the clients you were busily…*charming* during lunch today.'

'Taylor-Gant.' She supplied the name with her back still towards him so her frown was for her eyes only at the odd way he had used the word *charm*. 'We market their designer lingerie.'

'Do you wear it?'

He saw the flinch, was absolutely sure she was standing there with her eyes screwed shut—probably cursing herself for falling into that one? 'No,' she answered curtly, and opened the door.

'Then buy some,' he instructed. 'To market a product one should know exactly what it is you are marketing.'

'It isn't my job to know,' she protested.

'It is now,' he replied. 'I expect by the end of the week for you to have an opinion on their full range. And that, Miss Deyton,' he added for good measure, 'is exactly the kind of information the personal assistant to a corporate chairman is supposed to know.'

The door opened and closed, leaving him alone to smile at her hurried departure, very satisfyingly aware that she had left here feeling more confused than she had felt when she'd first walked in and found him here instead of Edward.

The game was on. He was in control. He didn't doubt it for a single moment. Natalia Deyton was his for the taking. He was actually enjoying himself—and within a week he intended to be enjoying himself a whole lot more…

CHAPTER TWO

STANDING on the other side of that closed door, Natalia was attempting to come to terms with what had just happened in there. It wasn't easy, simply because she didn't *know* what had happened—if you didn't count the disturbing impression that she had just indulged in the thorough seduction of all the senses.

And with Giancarlo Cardinale, of all people.

Her skin gave a flutter on a small inner shudder that helped release some of the tension out of her body. Not that she felt any better for it, she noted as she made herself walk across her office and then sank weakly down on the edge of her desk while she tried to get herself back together.

Giancarlo Cardinale. The name was playing over and over inside her head like a mantra, frightening, disturbing—exciting, alluring.

Oh, dear God. She closed her eyes only to find that, once again, his image was firmly imprinted on her retina. The dark hair and skin, the compelling brown velvet eyes that had held her captive even though she desperately hadn't wanted them to. Then there was his mouth—that terribly sensual mouth she could see drawing her own mouth towards it like metal to a magnet.

She could still feel the effects, still feel a warm, soft pulsing of needy flesh that brought her fingers up to cover her lips in an effort to stop the sensation. It didn't work, and if anything only seemed to make matters worse when she felt her blood begin to heat in the mere memory of what she had wanted his mouth to do to hers.

Then—no, she amended that. Her blood wasn't just growing hot, it was searing through her veins like pure radiation. Poisonous.

Poisonous? The word brought her hand snapping away from her mouth and her eyelids shooting open in shocked realisation of what she had just unwittingly done.

She had given the whole crazy experience a very accurate label, because, yes, Giancarlo Cardinale had to be poison—to her at any rate. Poison by passion, poison by desire, poison because she knew there could be no future in letting him come close. Yet she had a terrible feeling that she was going to let him close. That she simply was not going to be able to help herself.

The next shudder became a shiver, which brought goose-bumps standing out on her skin. The man was her enemy, she grimly reminded herself. *Any* member of the Cardinale clan was her enemy. But this one, this tall, dark, frighteningly sexy head of the house of Cardinale had the power to completely demolish her newly found belief in herself if he ever discovered just who it was he was dealing with.

Then there was Edward, she moved on to link one problem neatly with the other. Edward, of all people, knew the danger this situation was putting her in! So why had he done it? What the hell did he think he was playing at setting her up like this—and without any warning?

She jumped up, began pacing the floor, arms crossed, head bowed, eyebrows puckered by a frown as she tried to work out just what was going on here. It simply made no sense. Edward was her life. Both had sworn more than once that they couldn't bear to be without the other now. So why was he putting their relationship at risk like this?

A sudden thought had her spinning back to her desk. Hitching her behind onto its pale beech-wood top, she stretched over and tapped a button on her keyboard, which would activate her voice-mail. Surely Edward would not have gone blithely off on his cruise without leaving her some kind of explanation for all of this?

It was a real relief to hear his deep, rather hurried voice filling the room. 'Natalia, my dear. I have some news.'

In the very act of opening the door, Giancarlo Cardinale went perfectly still…

'I have very little time to explain this, so bear with me and concentrate,' Edward Knight instructed. 'Surprise— surprise!' He sounded tense and just a little anxious. 'Alegra and I are in Barbados, would you believe? And about to embark on a second-honeymoon cruise, care of— Giancarlo! The point is, he's arranged everything so right and tight that I hardly have time to make this call. But I had to warn you—he's coming there. He will be looking after the business while I am away. So you're going to have to watch your step with him. Watch what you do, watch what you say—and for goodness' sake don't fall in love with him! I need to know that my girl will still be there in one whole piece, waiting for me when I return.'

Natalia laughed, though it was a rather thick, self-deriding sound. Giancarlo on the other hand heard nothing even vaguely amusing in what Edward had said. His mouth was tight, his eyes hard. If Natalia had glanced round and seen him standing there, she would have run screaming for her life.

But she didn't turn, and Edward was still talking. 'Also I need you to do a few things for me before he arrives,' he explained.

'Too damn late,' she muttered.

'I have some personal papers locked in the safe—you

know the ones I mean,' he added brusquely. 'I would prefer Giancarlo not to set eyes on them. You know the combination—and so does Giancarlo now, because I was stupid enough to give it to him without thinking. So get all
my private stuff out of there before he has a chance to find
it, and keep it safe somewhere else for me until I come
home. Got to go now,' he announced hurriedly. 'Alegra is
glowering at me. I'm going to miss you. Be good while
I'm not there—'

The connection was broken. Behind her the door to
Edward's office was silently closing again, leaving Natalia
alone to mull over everything Edward had said—none of
which made her feel any happier with the situation. He'd
offered too little much too late and put their secret at risk
in the interim—which also told her that he still hadn't got
around to breaking the news about them to his wife.

'Oh, hell,' she sighed. When was he going to learn that
keeping secrets from the people you loved only made you
miserable?

Only in this particular case she had to concede he had
a valid reason for keeping silent. Alegra had taken enough
over the last tragic year—as Giancarlo himself had pointed
out. To discover that her husband was harbouring a dark,
dark secret was not the best silver wedding present he
could give his wife.

Then there were the papers he wanted her to get out of
his safe! How was she supposed to do that now the great
man was already firmly entrenched in Edward's office?

In Edward's office, she repeated and felt the dizzying
sway of her heart as it took her off on another tangent. A
tangent to do with Giancarlo Cardinale and Edward's other
instruction. Don't fall in love with him, he'd said. Well,
she saw no danger in that actuality happening.

But falling into bed with him was an entirely different thing.

Giancarlo was at Edward's desk working on a portable desktop computer when she took his coffee in. Freshly ground, Italian blend, just as he'd requested. He didn't look up, and she didn't speak as she carried the tray over to place it down by his elbow.

But just the sight of him sitting there was enough to make her nerve-ends crackle. I'll get over it, she told herself, using Edward's advice to strengthen her backbone. Like all surprise situations, the novelty always wears off after a while. It just requires overexposure.

Outside the bright February sun was just beginning to stream in through the window behind him now. And she couldn't resist pausing to watch the way the pale gold sunbeams poured light onto his black silk head and over his broad shoulders before filtering down his arms to the neatly kept tips of his long brown fingers.

Was there nothing about this man she didn't like? she wondered helplessly. Even the view of his nose from this new angle didn't seem to make it any less appealing. Her fingers itched to follow its arrogant contours, then slide lazily towards his—

Oh, stop it! she scolded herself and, without giving a second thought as to why she was doing it, she walked over to the window and angled the blinds so the light no longer hit him.

'I like the sun,' he remarked with an abruptness that had her turning to frown at the back of his bent head. 'My Sicilian blood has an unquenchable need for it.'

'Is your computer screen Sicilian too?' she quizzed, making light of his remark because she could see no reason for the sudden change in manner.

He didn't get the joke. 'Open the blinds,' he clipped, a

long finger stabbing almost angrily at a button on his keyboard that sent off into cyberspace a document he couldn't possibly have been able to read on his sun-blanched screen.

Without a word, she did as she was told, grimacingly aware that the atmosphere had most definitely turned frosty, though she hadn't the slightest idea as to why it had. See, the novelty is already wearing off, she told herself as she turned away from the window, feeling absolutely no chemical reaction at all to that particularly autocratic tone.

'Any messages?' he queried.

She had taken one step only and was suddenly freezing to the point that she actually stopped breathing. 'No,' she answered, having to force the lie up through her thickened throat.

'Not even from Edward?' he prompted. 'I expected him to put in one call at least, to check everything was all right here…'

Her pulse began to race. 'No, no call from Edward,' she denied.

Without any warning he sat back in the chair, then swung it round until he was facing her. With the sun now hitting him full in his face, his narrowed eyes seemed to glitter accusingly as they raked over her. Tension began to rise—a hard, tight, prickly kind of tension that had nothing to do with the man's sensual pull, but with the air of menace he seemed to be transmitting from every perfectly constructed cell.

'But if he rings, you will inform me immediately, hmm?' he probed, so softly that she hoped it was her own guilty conscience that was making her feel as if she was on trial here—and not that silken tone.

'Yes,' she lied yet again. 'Of course,' she then added

for good innocent measure, trying desperately to sound like the coolly detached and businesslike assistant she was supposed to be.

'Good.' Giancarlo smiled, but it wasn't a real smile—in fact it sent an icy chill chasing through her. Then without another word he swung back to the desk to continue with what he had been doing.

It was a silent dismissal she was more than happy to comply with, considering the huge lie she had just told him. Setting her tingling legs moving, she walked around the desk and began treading the expanse of grey carpet, which seemed to spread like a mine-infested ocean out in front of her, threatening to blow her lies up in her face each time she put a foot down.

She hated liars, she always had ever since the day she'd discovered how much her own mother had lied to her for most of her life. So to find herself doing it actually hurt a very sensitive part in her that she knew she was going to find difficult to pacify.

'What is Howard Fiske's extension number?'

This second question reached her at about halfway across the room. She told him. He murmured a thank-you. She walked on, thinking only of getting away so she could sit down somewhere away from prying eyes and grimly justify—if only to herself—what she had just done.

'And the combination to Edward's safe,' he then prompted. 'Do you know that also?'

At which point the excruciating tension she was beginning to feel threatened to swallow her whole. 'Don't you know it?' she asked, frowning because she was recalling what Edward had said.

'Edward wrote it down for me,' he confirmed. 'But I do not have it on me right at this moment.'

Relief fluttered through her. If he hadn't got the combination with him, then she had time to get Edward's papers out of harm's way—so long as she could grab the opportunity to do so.

'I can't help you there, I'm sorry,' she apologised, comforting herself with the weak excuse that her reply hadn't been a full lie—only a half one. She *couldn't* help him, and she *was* sorry. But she was feeling as if the combination were presently burning itself in block letters across her guilty face and all he had to do was get her to turn and face him so that he could read it!

'Maybe Howard knows it,' he murmured.

'Maybe he does,' she agreed, sure in the knowledge that Howard *didn't* know. Then she whipped quickly through the door before he could come up with any more uncomfortable questions...

Giancarlo Cardinale watched her go with his head fizzing on the very edge of a violent eruption. Lying little witch, he was thinking angrily. Lying, cheating, *beautiful* witch! he tagged on hotly as he watched that tight rear-end disappear through the door and felt his fingers itch to go chasing after it.

'You will get yours, Miss Deyton,' he promised. 'One day soon you will most certainly get yours.'

Picking up the phone, he punched in Howard Fiske's number. Five minutes later he was putting the phone down again and feeling downright miffed on so many fronts that he couldn't make his mind up which took priority.

Howard didn't know the combination to Edward's safe, which didn't really surprise him, or the deceitful Miss Deyton would have gone to pieces, he was sure. But Miss Deyton had not gone to pieces. She had tossed off her airy replies with guileful ease! Which meant he was going to have to keep a very keen eye on her if he didn't want that safe opening today without him knowing it.

And Howard himself was another problem he was going to have to deal with. Having fed Giancarlo all the ammunition he needed to do something about Edward's little office affair, Howard had expected him to come here and get rid of Natalia without any compunction. Now the mean-mouthed swine was angry because Giancarlo was refusing to play it his way.

What was it with Howard, anyway? he suddenly asked himself as he got up to go and stand by the window. Did the man fancy Natalia himself—was that it? Was his attitude sour grapes because Edward was enjoying something Howard would like to enjoy himself?

Something hot began to burn in his stomach, and he knew exactly what was causing it. It was the sudden image of not one, but two, middle-aged lechers pawing her smooth white flesh, while she let them—because she liked it.

His hand snaked up, and with a violent tug on the pullcord he cut out that image by snapping shut the blinds he had insisted Natalia opened.

Petty or what? he asked himself. Petty—yes, he admitted. Angry—yes. With Edward, with Howard—with *himself* for all wanting the same woman!

Well, one third of the competition had already been removed from the picture. And another third could go the same way quick enough, he decided as he turned to snatch up the phone again.

Ten minutes after *that* particular call, and he was beginning to feel back in control. By tomorrow Howard Fiske and his filthy mouth would be flying to Milan to spend a couple of weeks smouldering in frustration beneath the wing of Giancarlo Cardinale's second in command, learning how his job should be done. By the time he was due back, Natalia Deyton would be so much Giancarlo's woman that Howard would only have to glance at her to know that the problem had been dealt with—Giancarlo's way.

Yes, he felt a whole lot better about that little scenario...

She'd forgotten to take the requested files in to him. Seeing them sitting there, still neatly stacked on her desk where she had placed them before taking in his coffee, made her want to hit something in utter frustration—because it meant she was now going to have to go back in there.

And she just didn't want to. She didn't want to face another barrage of awkward questions, or face the man himself, for that matter! Giancarlo was like a ride on a roller coaster, she likened. One minute rocketing her into a steep dive through all the senses, the next he was hurling her into a corkscrew twist, making her struggle with her own guilty secrets. It was all so very precarious that she dared not so much as breathe in case she caused the whole thing to come crashing down around her!

The intercom on her desk began to beep. 'Those files, Miss Deyton?' drawled her tormentor with a coolness that did nothing to ease her turmoil.

That sexy voice should be X-rated, she decided as she flicked a switch to acknowledge the reminder with what she hoped was a matching cool. Then, taking a deep breath, she gathered up the armful of files and began walking back towards that connecting door, which was beginning to resemble the entrance to a torture chamber...

The moment she stepped through it, she sensed the change in the atmosphere. The blinds had been drawn, blocking out the shafts of sunlight which had given the room such a sharp edge before.

And he wasn't where she'd expected him to be, she realised, glancing at the empty chair behind the desk before beginning to scan the new softer light until she located him over on the other side of the room. He was sitting comfortably stretched out on one of Edward's soft grey leather sofas with his dark head thrown back, his eyes closed and with his feet propped up on the low beechwood coffee-table. The tray she had brought in earlier now resided beside his feet—and, like his jacket, his tie had now disappeared and the top couple of buttons on his shirt had been tugged free.

Was he intending to complete a full strip before the afternoon was over? she found herself speculating sarcastically.

Then wished she hadn't thought such a stupid thing when, on a sudden rush to the head, she found herself picturing him stretched out there naked. Brown skin, long, powerfully muscled legs, a hard-toned, superbly built masculine torso, she saw in that single fevered flash of a moment. But it did not stop there. Oh, no, because she was also picturing the look in his eyes as he waited for her to join him in the self-same naked state.

'Come and join me,' he murmured.

She almost jumped out of her skin! As it was she reacted violently enough to send the top file sliding off the pile so it slithered to the floor in a spill of white paper. In a flurry of pure wit-scattering dismay, she bent to place the rest of the files on the floor then began gathering together the papers with fingers that had lost the ability to co-ordinate.

How could you—how *could* you? She was railing at herself, relieved to have the diversion so she could hide her flaming cheeks, which she knew without a doubt were displaying every naughty thought running through her wicked head!

Never *ever* had she indulged in wild fantasies over any man—so why start now with this one of all the men she could have chosen?

'Here, let me...'

A pair of black leather shoes appeared in her vision. Then a pair of dark silk worsted-covered knees as he bent into a very male squat. She felt ready to self-incinerate when her eyes began flickering along his inner thighs. Dragging them away again, she made a reckless grab at a piece of paper—as a long brown hand did the same.

Skin touched skin. Electricity went crackling up her arm with such clamouring speed that it almost knocked her right off balance! She let out a gasp; there was no containing it, nor the sharp way that her head came up. Blue eyes clashed helplessly with deep dark brown.

After that there was stillness, a complete and utter stillness with hand touching hand and eyes holding eyes, swapping a knowledge that neither was doing anything to disguise.

No, her common sense was trying to advise her. Don't let this happen. It's wrong, it's dangerous, it's too darn complicated to warrant taking the risk.

But he's so irresistible, her weaker self whispered. Exciting, beguiling, utterly compelling. She even felt herself leaning closer—just as she had done the last time she had looked deeply into his eyes...

Somewhere in the distance a phone began to ring. It was her salvation. And, good grief, but she needed saving! she acknowledged as, on a flurry of embarrassment, she withdrew her hand and scrambled to her feet, then fled back into her own office, leaving him still squatting there, with his dark eyes following her every single step of the way.

The call was an internal query that took all her powers of concentration to answer without sounding drunk. By the time she came back, the files had been stacked on the coffee-table and Giancarlo Cardinale was poring over the contents of one of them.

'Come and sit down,' he instructed without a single inflection in his tone to so much as hint at what had just passed between them.

She moved on legs that were still feeling weak and unsteady, over to the sofa on the opposite side of the table.

'No, not there,' he said. 'Sit here, next to me so we can look at these together.'

Together, she repeated to herself. What a buzzword. What a provocatively tantalising buzzword. And as she moved to perch herself stiffly on the cushion next to his she found herself wishing that the man were as ugly as sin.

'Coffee?' he offered.

'I don't drink it,' she politely refused.

An eyebrow tweaked as he scanned the typed print on the piece of paper he was reading. 'What—never?' he asked, but she had a feeling the raised eyebrow was mocking the stiff way she was sitting there.

'Sometimes—after dinner maybe.' She shrugged, stubbornly deciding that it was time to take every single word he spoke at its absolute face value. No hearing hidden meanings, no looking for anything other than a professional boss-assistant relationship.

'A cup-of-tea girl,' he presumed, placing one piece of paper aside to pick up another.

'I prefer water, if you must know,' she told him.

'A woman with simple tastes, then.'

'Yes.' She nodded—very firmly because she *was* a woman of simple tastes. And Giancarlo Cardinale was not simple at all. He was a rare delicacy only the very rich or the very reckless would consider trying. She was neither rich nor reckless. In fact, she was the most cautious person she knew!

Which only made her reaction to Giancarlo Cardinale all the more perturbing. It just wasn't like her.

'Now…' he said on a complete change of manner '…explain to me why this company needs the skills of marketing experts when the product they produce virtually sells itself…'

Peering over his arm, she saw the famous Fillens logo, and smiled ruefully at his comment. 'Geoffrey Fillen and Edward were at school together,' she explained. 'Fillens have been using Edward's marketing skills for as long as he has been in business.'

'Ah, the old school network.' Giancarlo grimaced understandingly. 'Lucky Edward. Does the business from this company also come via the same route?' he asked, indicating towards a different file.

After that, she became engrossed in a lesson on the astuteness of this man's business mind as he began picking out the base-root foundation upon which Edward had built his company.

And as the afternoon wore on she found herself becoming more and more fascinated by Edward's brother-in-law as he displayed qualities that by far outweighed the merely physical. He was shrewd, he was quick, he was incredibly logical when it came to matters of business.

He possessed a low-pitched and easy telephone manner that clearly kept his listeners safely assured that, though he might not be where they wanted him to be, he was still accessible and in control, with his finger most firmly on the pulse of everything beneath the Cardinale Group umbrella.

She even knew when he was talking to his secretary because his tone grew firmer, sharper, more commanding—though she didn't understand a word because he was speaking in Italian. A language that worked on the senses like alcohol, sluicing out tensions and replacing them with warm, soft feelings of—

Oh, no, not again. With a jerk she fixed her attention on the stream of notes he'd had her taking. The phone went down—and rang again almost immediately. Without a pause he switched from Italian to English, and began a discussion about corporate profit projections that left her completely flummoxed.

Dynamic was the word she was toying with when he suddenly sat down beside her again. Heat sizzled between them, but she grimly ignored the stomach-curling effect it had on her.

By five o'clock, open files lay scattered all about them and the coffee-table, and the lights were on to supplement the loss of sunlight seeping in through the blinds.

Natalia was beginning to fade a little, but Giancarlo wasn't. Like a human dynamo, the more he found to delve into, the more invigorated he became.

So another hour went by, and she was kneeling on the carpet by the coffee-table, carefully feeding paper back into the files he had scrutinised and finished with, when yet another phone call took him striding back to the desk.

The moment he began speaking Natalia was aware of the difference in this call from all of the other calls, no matter what language he was speaking. This one was being carried out in Italian—a warm, soft, intimate Italian loaded down with so much sensual promise that she didn't doubt for a moment just whom it was he was speaking to.

A lover. It had to be. And as she sank back onto her ankles feeling very odd suddenly, as if someone had just punched her in the stomach, she couldn't believe that she hadn't so much as considered the prospect of his having a lover in his life.

Well, that's fine. It's okay, she tried telling herself. In fact it suited her very well that he had someone else to concentrate his sexual interest upon! But inside she burned and squirmed with that nasty hot thing called jealous resentment, which only got worse the more 'cara mia's and 'mia bella amore's she caught interspersing his husky-toned conversation.

It seemed a good point for her to make her exit, she decided, slamming the last file back down on the stack with more violence than was necessary.

The sound it made had him glancing up, but his dark gaze was hazed by distraction, the kind of distraction that set her heart thudding on a burst of good old-fashioned anger. The kind of anger that had her coming to her feet and walking towards the door without bothering to announce her departure.

'Going somewhere?' his silken voice came sliding after her.

She glanced back, saw him leaning there against Edward's desk, with a hand clamped over the telephone mouthpiece—and a glint in his eyes that she just didn't like.

It came too close to sexual arousal for her fastidious sensitivities. Couldn't the man wait until he had his privacy before indulging in that kind of conversation? He was even daring to peruse her figure as if it belonged to the woman who was arousing him, she noticed in affront.

'It's late,' she bit out. 'In case you haven't noticed. We seem to have finished here, so I'll leave you to it.'

With that she walked out, firmly closing the door behind her with absolutely no suspicion that the man she had left on the other side of it was now slowly replacing the phone

on its rest, with a smile on his face that could only be
described as—triumphant...

He was getting to her—really getting to her! It felt pretty
good. He even gave the phone a light tap as if in thanks
for its help. Then the smile cracked into a full-blooded
grin when he thought of Serena, his best friend's wife, who
had just laughingly threatened to tell Fredo if Giancarlo
didn't stop speaking to her in that seductive tone of voice!

The phone rang again. He picked it up, knowing exactly
who was going to be on the other end of it. 'Fredo—all is
fair in love and war,' he announced before the other man
could get a word in. 'And before you ask, no, my war is
not being waged against your beautiful wife...'

CHAPTER THREE

'*BUON GIORNO*, Miss Deyton,' Giancarlo greeted briskly as he strode in the next morning. 'You had a pleasant evening, I hope, and are feeling rested enough to begin a whole new day?'

No, she hadn't, and no, she wasn't, but it was all too obvious that he'd had more than enough of both, she noted, viewing his irritatingly upbeat manner through heavily jaundiced eyes.

Everything about him appeared thoroughly revitalised from the brightness in his tone to the healthy sheen of his olive-toned skin. Clearly burning the candle at both ends had only an invigorating effect on him. Even his clothes looked sharp enough to draw blood if you touched them, she thought as she ran those same eyes over his steel-grey suit with its matching colour shirt and silk tie.

Whereas she felt wrecked because she had done nothing but wage war with herself right through the evening and into the night. Troubled by her lies, troubled by her attraction to him and more than troubled by the uncontrollable way her imagination had insisted on drawing lurid pictures of him locked in the arms of some gorgeous Italian who possessed all the sensual expertise a man like Giancarlo Cardinale would expect from the woman he allowed into his bed!

'A Ms Delucca just called,' she informed him frostily. 'To complain about you leaving this morning, without saying thank you.'

'Ah, Serena,' he murmured smilingly—a smile that be-

39

came a disgustingly rakish full-blooded grin, which showed no sign whatever of any embarrassment at having his private life put on show like this. 'I will apologise later. But first we have some things to do that will—'

He stopped. Went still, seemed to stiffen slightly, then suddenly lost all of that rakish humour. 'How long have you been in?' he demanded suddenly.

'About five minutes,' she replied, suddenly very aware of how finely she'd timed getting Edward's papers out of the safe before Giancarlo had arrived. The day did not officially start for another half an hour and she'd really thought she'd had plenty of time. As it was, the darned man had virtually caught her with her hand in the safe!

But as far as *he* was concerned, she might not have got around to removing her coat yet, but she *had* collected the post and checked for emails—plus taken a call from his current mistress!

'Do you have a problem with that, Mr Cardinale?' she demanded, having already come to the decision at some point in the early hours of the morning that she was not going to let him turn her inside out for two days on the run!

He didn't answer, but he was frowning darkly. And if she could glean any consolation from that frown then it was in the knowledge that his irritatingly upbeat mood had so obviously collapsed.

'Take your coat off and come into my office,' he instructed, jumping into autocratic mode with a snap to his tone that sent her hackles up.

'Yes, sir,' she replied, using frost to his bite.

He muttered something she didn't catch, then strode through the connecting door before slamming it shut behind him.

She allowed herself an exaggerated wince, then began

removing her camel-coloured full-length cashmere coat and soft lilac scarf at a speed that confirmed her determination not to be bullied. So she took her time settling it on its hanger, then took another few moments to smooth down the fabric of her calf-length black pinstriped suit. She had chosen to wear this particular suit because it showed less leg and the tailored jacket fastened right up to its mandarin collar. Her hair was up as usual, neatly secured by a black shell clasp, and her make-up was so underplayed it might not even be there.

If anyone could look at her and even vaguely suggest that she was asking for the kind of looks Signor Cardinale had treated her to yesterday, she would call them liars! But she was not seeing that all she had done with her severe cover-up was incite the imagination to wonder what was being hidden...

Which was exactly what Giancarlo began thinking about from the moment she stepped into his office. Natalia's hair glistened like polished copper, her skin sheened like a pearl. Her body moved with the sensual grace of a born siren—and her eyes would be cutting him into two pieces if he were made of glass.

The woman was not of this world, he grimly decided. She was all fire and ice and dangerous witchery. She filled him with the primitive urge to go over there, pull her into his arms and kiss her senseless.

And she knew it. Look at her! he growled to himself. Standing there with her chin up, just daring him to try it!

'We are changing location,' he announced right off the top of his head and with no idea of what he was talking about. All he knew was that he wanted her out of this place before she found a way to get her sticky fingers into Edward's safe. It had almost ruined his day to come in here this morning and find that she had got here before him. He seemed to have misplaced the piece of paper with the combination number that Edward had given him, and six long weeks of wondering when she was going to grab enough time away from him unseen to crack the darn safe were more than he was prepared to cope with. Though he was going to have his work cut out trying to come up with a valid excuse for making such an impulsive announcement, he admitted.

Still, it had been worth it just to see that cold, haughty expression she was wearing this morning collapse into a flurry of confusion.

'What?' she choked out as if he'd spoken in a strange language.

If he could have any wish granted right now, it would be to have that sensational gasping mouth fixed permanently to his own hungry mouth.

'I have decided I cannot work here,' he continued, thinking on his feet and glad he was good at it. 'It is too complicated trying to run this company as well as my own from here. You saw yourself how much time I spent on the telephone yesterday when I should have been devoting my energies to what is wrong right here.'

Wrong right here... Natalia stared at the hand he was using to punctuate the point with long fingertips stabbing into Edward's desk, and felt a horrid little flutter of alarm slither down her backbone. 'Wha-what's wrong here?' she stammered out warily.

'Everything,' he replied. And she wasn't even wearing any lipstick, he noted. Did she know he couldn't stand the taste of lipstick? 'Even the little information I gleaned from the files yesterday was enough to tell me that this place is in deep trouble.' She blinked, and he grimaced because that part at least was the ugly truth. 'The premises may have been thoroughly modernised but its business practices are positively archaic, so I am about to do something about it.'

'But—you can't do that!' she protested. 'It isn't your place to mess with Edward's business!'

'I can do anything I want, Miss Deyton,' he corrected her with a haughty incision. 'I own controlling stock here, in case you have forgotten. When I injected a large amount of cash into this place last year, Edward's brief was to completely modernise. He seems to have gone as far as refurbishing the premises—and no damned farther.'

'His son died…'

'I am aware of that,' Giancarlo clipped out. He felt his face harden when he recalled where Edward's energies had gone to salve his grief for his dead son, when they could have been salved by continuing the job he had begun right here, where it mattered. But he hadn't done that, and everything at Knight's had simply stagnated while Edward indulged himself in a bit of womanly comfort.

This woman's womanly comforts. Fire flared up from his heart, diverted to his eyes and spat sparks out over Natalia Deyton. 'Grief is no excuse for tardy business practices,' he proclaimed with what even he knew was a gross lack of sympathy.

'So what is it you intend to do?' she asked in a tone meant to slay him for his insensitivity.

'Bring in my team of experts,' he said, glancing down at his watch and wondering if he could pull this off in the time space he was gunning for. 'They will arrive late this afternoon and set up a six-week re-educating programme that will haul the staff here into this century. Howard Fiske already knows about it,' he added with what he now saw as a clever bit of unwitting pre-planning. 'He is, as we speak, flying to my head office in Milan, to begin his own re-education on how I expect my executives to conduct themselves.'

'I thought you were Sicilian,' Natalia murmured, so out of context in his point of view that it stopped his train of thought completely.

'What has that got to do with anything?' he demanded.

'You said Milan,' she explained with a shrug meant to convey mild indifference. But in truth even she didn't understand why she said such a stupid thing. 'I just presumed you lived and worked in Sicily. Edward said...'

She faded out, seeing by his sudden narrowing expression that he didn't like what was being said here.

'Edward said—what?' he prompted grittily.

Another shrug and she was beginning to feel just a little hunted. 'I only remember him remarking once, about your home in—in Trápani, I think he said,' she answered warily. 'He m-made it sound very—beautiful.'

If she'd been looking for a diversion with that last remark, she didn't achieve it. 'Quite cosy little chats you two must have indulged in to reach the point where they included me,' he remarked. 'Maybe we should sit down and compare notes some time. See if his references to you were as—interesting...'

His tone was cold, and she'd gone quite pale. But the very thought of her having this kind of conversation about him with Edward set his teeth on edge...

Natalia, on the other hand, was kicking herself for starting this at all. She knew his comment about comparing notes was merely his way of getting back at her, because Edward would *never* have discussed her with Giancarlo. Not during this lifetime anyway.

But she was genuinely regretful for invading what Giancarlo clearly saw as his privacy. And despite knowing she should leave it alone, the words of explanation came anyway. 'Edward was missing his son,' she gently explained. 'He seemed to need to talk about him so I let him. Your home in Sicily came up because I gained the impression that Marco used to spend a great deal of his time there with you. So it was perhaps natural for Edward to refer to that.'

He had stopped looking at her, his eyes becoming hidden beneath the long sweep of his lashes. Anxious because she was concerned that she'd only managed to upset him further, she took an impulsive couple of steps closer to the desk behind which he was standing. 'Please don't think he discussed you personally, because he didn't,' she assured.

To her surprise, he smiled, albeit grimly. 'I was ten years old when Edward married Alegra. Two years later Marco arrived. We were more like brothers than uncle and nephew. When he died last year, we all—went to pieces a little. I have not been back to Sicily since he died there, for instance. Alegra sank deep inside herself, while Edward...' he paused, seemed about to say something else, then, on a short sigh, changed his mind '...Edward found his own means of escape,' he clipped out. 'Which is why this place has been left to stagnate over the last year. But now it's time to do something about it,' he added on a firmer, brisker note. 'So we will begin by getting in my team of experts to knock his staff into shape while Edward himself devotes some long-overdue time to patching up his ailing marriage.'

Why it seemed as though he had turned that last comment into a threat, Natalia didn't understand. But as for the rest of it—oh, she understood it all far more than he would ever know. Marco had been visiting Giancarlo in Sicily when the tragic accident had happened. Young, reckless and with his whole life ahead of him, Marco had taken Giancarlo's Ferrari out without permission, lost control of the powerful machine, and crashed it, killing himself as he'd done so.

Those of his family left behind were inconsolable. Directly after the funeral in Sicily, Giancarlo had flown off the island and disappeared for weeks somewhere no one could find him. Alegra had gone into deep mourning. No one had been able to get near her. She'd spent hours in Marco's bedroom here in London. It had become a shrine, Edward told her once. A sad, torturous, sacred shrine.

And Edward? Well, Edward's story was equally as sad though not quite as wretched as the others. Because he'd found her, Natalia admitted. In her he'd found a link with his son and someone into whom he could divert all that painful love he had festering inside him.

'He doesn't even have a picture of Marco in here,' Giancarlo grated, with a contempt aimed at Edward that hid a lot of his own pain, Natalia suspected.

'It's in the safe,' she said. 'He couldn't bear to look at it, so he put it away...'

The safe, Giancarlo repeated bitterly to himself. What else had Edward got hidden in his damned safe that he didn't want him to look at? Pictures of his wife in happier times? Pictures of his lovely mistress who'd helped him to live again while the rest of them still floundered in guilt and misery?

The phone began to ring. It was a relief to have something to take his mind off the black anger suddenly consuming him. To hell with Natalia Deyton, he decided as he snatched up the receiver. To hell with his seduction plan! He'd had enough. She was out.

And as soon as this call was over. He never wanted to set eyes on Edward's mistress again if he could help it!

It was his second in command calling from Milan, wanting to know what he was supposed to do with Howard Fiske when he arrived. As he began biting out orders, Natalia turned as if to leave him to it.

'Stay,' he growled.

She stopped, then turned her head to look at him questioningly over her shoulder. The eyes were sad, the blue irises darkened mirrors that reflected the distress of what they had been discussing.

Had Edward received that same look when he'd opened up his grief to Natalia Deyton? If he had then it was no wonder he'd used her as his escape from misery, Giancarlo decided. Because he could feel himself being drawn towards the same exquisite means of escape.

For vengeance, he added, recalling why all of this had started. Vengeance for putting at risk what was left of his sister's broken heart, by seducing her husband. Well, an eye for an eye—the Sicilian way, he reminded himself. Or, in this case, seduction for seduction. It was so very appropriate...

The game was back on. He suddenly felt better, and sat down in the chair to begin a more lazily sarcastic conversation with his caller, while casually waving Natalia into the other chair.

She didn't comply. He wasn't surprised. He had seen by her body language, from the moment he'd walked in this morning, that she had decided to take him on.

He liked the idea of that. It added spice to the chase and gave his mood another lift that did wonders for his testosterone levels. And he even set himself a rather titillating deadline, which involved him tasting her lovely mouth before the day was over.

'Right, that's it,' he said, switching from Italian to English the moment he put down the phone. 'All the arrangements are confirmed. My people will be here by late afternoon. What I need from you now is a tour of all departments, so I can make the initial assessment on what they are going to be required to do.'

'I still don't think this is right without Edward's agreement,' Natalia informed him.

'Your protest has been noted,' he coolly acknowledged, and glanced at his watch before coming to his feet. 'Time to move,' he announced. 'We have a lot to get through before we stop for lunch. Then we should, with a bit of luck, have some new premises to look over this afternoon.'

'We?' Natalia prompted. 'What has your choice in new premises got to do with me?'

'Since you will be relocating right along with me—' he shrugged '—I automatically assumed you would like to look your new workplace over.'

But Natalia didn't want to relocate with him! In fact the very suggestion filled her with utter dismay! 'But my job is here!' she protested. 'I am *needed* here! Edward—'

'Your job, Miss Deyton,' he cut in coldly, 'is wherever or whatever I decide it is. And why do I get the impression that you suspect my every move is designed to actually harm this company?' he added grimly.

When he put it like that she began to feel rather stupid, because he was right and she did suspect him of—something, though she had to confess she didn't know what that something was.

'I'm sorry,' she sighed, making a climb-down she knew she really had no choice about. 'But you've been here for less than twenty-four hours and already you're planning to turn the place upside down!'

'Upside down is better than the way it stands at present,' he returned with contempt, then released a sigh of his own because her climb-down had made him realise that his confrontational stance was not helping his cause. 'Listen,' he said, aiming for a more conciliatory tone. 'Allowing me to turn this business around while Edward is safely out of the way where he can't worry is doing him a favour, believe me. And to make it work in the short time allowed, I need you to work with me, not against me. Is that too much to ask—for Edward's sake—?'

Her stubborn stance was faltering. He could see it happening in the frown that clouded her face. 'Okay,' she said heavily. 'What is it you need me to do?'

With a surrender like that, he didn't hesitate in consolidating it. 'I need someone I can trust working alongside me, and, since Edward clearly trusts you, then you have to be my obvious choice,' he explained, watching his carefully chosen words work their expected magic.

She was hooked. He had her...

'So,' he continued, 'while my people come in here and turn this place around, you and I will move out so they can do their job without feeling me breathing down their necks. What I need from you is your secretarial skills and your input on any decision-making I may be required to do regarding Knight's.'

'What about *my* re-education?' Natalia questioned dryly, trying to make light of what had turned out to be yet another heavy interview. But the moment she saw that gleam enter his eyes she knew she'd said the wrong thing.

'You think I am not up to the task?' he probed silkily.

And it was back, just like that. From clever negotiator to lazy seducer in one smooth movement. His eyes feathered over her and her skin began to flutter. He paused at certain relevant locations and caused absolute mayhem.

Stop it! she wanted to snap. But 'stop it!' would only encourage him into being more provocative. So she clamped her lips shut, gritted her teeth tightly together behind them and said absolutely nothing.

Though what really made her teeth grit together was the warm, soft laugh he emitted as he walked around the desk. 'Coming?' he queried innocently and strode towards the door with that smile still working.

She followed because she really had no option. But she couldn't say that she was pleased with what had transpired in here today. As she entered her own office the telephone began to ring. Diverting towards her desk, she picked up the receiver. Ten seconds later she was gritting her teeth yet again, and holding the receiver out to him.

'The lady who rang you earlier, sir,' she announced with frosty formality.

The mocking smile on his face warmed into pure pleasure. He took the phone and Natalia only just escaped their fingers brushing by a fine hair's breadth. 'Ah, *buon giorno, mia bella amore...*'

The rest she shut her ears to and instead walked out of the room and into the executive washroom, where she spent a few seething moments bringing her composure back into line. By the time she entered her office again, he was busy scrawling something on her note-pad, and the telephone was back on its rest.

Arrangements for their next date? she wondered acidly, watching him tear off the piece of paper, fold it and slide it into his jacket pocket.

'Right, that tour,' he said, and began walking straight towards her.

She held her ground out of sheer cussedness. It was a stupid stand to make because he simply slid a hand around her waist and turned her to walk with him. Her breathing failed, her body started singing, and her mind went blank in response.

That hand—that hand...was the only chant playing over and over in an empty chasm of dark self-awareness.

'Where do we begin?' he enquired so innocently she could have screamed because he knew exactly what the feel of his hand on her waist was doing to her!

'The accounts department seems a good place.' She was rather pleased by how smoothly her voice came out.

'Before we go in—' he said, swinging her deftly up against the wall, then coming to stand directly over her. She was suddenly faced full on with his wide chest, and it took all her control not to start breathing faster.

'This is a delicate situation,' he murmured, seeming to have no idea how appropriate she was finding the comment. 'It is essential that you and I present a united front when we begin breaking the news to the staff here about what is about to happen. We must be relaxed, congenial and seem as one in our confidence that what we are proposing will be for their good as well as the company. This way there is a chance that they will be a help to my staff when they arrive and not a hindrance, you understand me?'

Natalia nodded, and wished he would move back a bit.

'We will not give the impression that I am here to scrutinise or criticise,' he continued. 'But all the same we will be doing both. You can do this, do you think?'

'Play the cheerful spy?' she said, making the fatal mistake of lifting her chin to send him a rueful smile. A smile that died on her lips when she caught his expression. She looked away again quickly, but not quickly enough to save herself from the disturbing glow she had seen burning in his eyes. 'I can't say it's my favourite role,' she added distractedly.

'But for their sakes, you will do it anyway?'

Their sakes. 'Yes,' she said, accepting that she was going to have to trust him to do what he had said he was going to do here, while taking into consideration the feelings of the people he would be dealing with.

'Good.' He moved back. Her relief to have no part of him touching her was so profound that she almost wilted into the carpet.

For the next couple of hours they paced from department to department. She introduced him to everyone individually, and, in typical Italian style, he charmed them all from the junior receptionist upwards. And in the charming gleaned so much information out of each and every one of them that Natalia was rather shell-shocked, by the end of it, as to how many people working there had been willing if not desperate for the changes Giancarlo was proposing.

'Right, let's get out of here,' he said eventually, and began striding across the reception area towards the doors, without waiting to see if she was following.

He was angry, she acknowledged, and couldn't really blame him for feeling that way. The long list of personal grievances, which had been aired here this morning, was enough to incense anyone with a reasonable grasp of good business practice. And whatever else she doubted about Giancarlo Cardinale, she did not doubt his business integrity.

Poor Edward, she thought sadly as she stepped outside to find Giancarlo had already hailed a cab and was opening the door ready for her to precede him into it.

Edward had no idea how low morale was amongst his staff and would have been deeply hurt if he'd been here today to discover what Giancarlo had so slickly uncovered.

So maybe it was right that Edward wasn't going to be here to see the transformation of his precious company, she concluded.

He waited until they were driving towards Kensington

before making any comment. 'Things are even worse than I envisaged,' he said.

'I know,' she agreed. There was nothing to be gained from pretending otherwise.

'How long have you known?'

Her shrug conveyed her reluctance to answer. 'Don't ask me to criticise Edward because I will not,' she told him and turned her head to stare bleakly out of the cab's side window.

'You admire the fact that he has run his own company into the ground?' The snap in his tone was laced with sarcasm.

Natalia kept her face turned away and said nothing in answer. For what could she say in Edward's defence that would not be betraying his darkest secrets? She couldn't. It was as simple as that. Edward's pride was just too important to her.

Strange, she mused, how one person could become the axis your life revolved around in such a short length of time. This time six months ago she hadn't even known of Edward's existence. This time six months ago she had been alone and sad, and seeing nothing bright in her future to make her feel any better, then—wham—everything had changed with one single glance across a café table.

It could still make her heart leap just to think of him, think of his loving face and his loving eyes, and that silly expression that would come over both, which would say without words—I still can't believe that you belong to me.

But she did, and nothing—nothing in this big world was ever going to take that away from her.

So her silence remained a wall she maintained between them as they travelled. Whatever Giancarlo was thinking about that silence did not really affect her. The man professed to care about Edward. And she did trust him to do what was best for his brother-in-law's company. But she would never trust him with Edward's heart, for it would take another man who had been hurt as deeply as Edward to understand its secrets.

The restaurant was a small, smart, popular place serving Italian cuisine. And Giancarlo was known there. The proprietor himself escorted them to their reserved table conversing with Giancarlo in their native language as they went. But she could tell the man beside her was in no mood to share polite conversation with anyone right now.

The proprietor helped her into her seat. Giancarlo sat down opposite. Menus were produced. A bottle of sparkling water appeared from seemingly nowhere. And the telling fact that Giancarlo must have ordered it, since no other table had the same thing, made her aware that, whatever else was going on inside his head, he could still call up the short, throw-away conversation about her drinking preferences, which they'd had yesterday.

At last the proprietor took his effusive leave. Giancarlo heaved out a sigh that made her smile in wry understanding of its necessity. He saw the smile—and matched it with one of his own. 'He is Sicilian; I supposed you guessed it. We come from the same village.'

Only you lived on top of the hill while he lived at the bottom, she presumed simply because of the proprietor's constant if metaphorical cap-doffing.

'Don't expect to use that,' he warned, arching a mocking brow at the menu she was holding. 'For I think we are about to be treated to the full repertoire of Sicilian cuisine.'

'Good or bad?' she asked, made curious by his rueful expression.

'Edward hates it,' he replied and instantly had her withdrawing back behind her protective wall…

* * *

Giancarlo saw it happen, sat back in his seat with a heavy sigh and lifted a long-fingered hand up to his tie knot as if he was going to loosen it with an impatient yank, then changed his mind and dropped the hand to his lap instead. 'Your loyalty to him becomes you, Miss Deyton. But have you tried to consider that loyalty in this case may well be misplaced?'

'You clearly don't like him very much. I do, which means we have a conflict of opinion that does not encourage an exchange in confidences.'

'You are mistaken,' he corrected. 'I am very fond of Edward. I just dislike the fact that he seems hell-bent on destroying everything he used to hold so dear.'

'Grief does that to some people,' she replied, having no idea that, in making that comment, Giancarlo was talking about more than just Edward's crumbling business.

'You said that with the conviction of experience,' he remarked, following the shadow which crossed her face.

'My mother died fourteen months ago,' she confessed, keeping her lashes lowered so he wouldn't see the pain in her eyes. 'Unexpectedly, like Marco,' she added. 'And even you know the kind of effect that shock and grief can have on you.'

'I didn't use it as an excuse to neglect my responsibilities,' he grimly pointed out.

Well, I did, and Edward did—as did Giancarlo's own sister, Alegra—though she was sure he didn't want to hear that, Natalia mused grimly, and reached for the bottle of water, mainly for something to do to hide the sudden heaviness of heart she was feeling.

'And your father—?' he asked, wondering what he had to say about his twenty-five-year-old daughter's affair with a man almost twice her age.

To Giancarlo's surprise her skin went as pale as the cloth covering the table.

'My mother never married.'

He beat her to the water bottle by a mere hair's breadth brush of their fingers. She snatched her hand away to place it on her lap where her nails curled into a skin-piercing fist while she concentrated on the sparkling water he was pouring into two wineglasses in the taut hope that he wouldn't ask any more probing questions.

He didn't. Being as astute as any red-blooded man deeply interested in the woman he meant to thoroughly seduce in the very near future, he realised her reply was her polite way of saying that she never knew her father.

So, with her mother gone, had she begun casting her eyes around looking for someone to fill the hole that had opened up in her life, and found the perfect substitute in a never-known father-figure like Edward?

It all seemed very plausible suddenly—forgivable even—though he had no intention whatsoever of going down that road simply because it would lead him away from what he was now wanting for too many reasons to count.

Not quite liking what that admission was saying to him, he picked up the wineglass and took a deep swallow—forgetting what was actually in the glass!

His expression was so comically disgusted that Natalia forgot to stay aloof and found herself laughing. 'You didn't have to have water just because I do,' she gently pointed out.

'I was trying to impress you with my temperance!' he threw back accusingly. 'And all you do is laugh!'

'I don't need impressing,' she told him with the laughter still warming her eyes.

His own grew still. 'Oh, yes, you do,' he insisted, and

watched her jump straight back behind her wall as the temperature between them came back to a steady simmer.

I'll have you, Natalia Deyton, he vowed. By fair means or foul, I *will* have you...

CHAPTER FOUR

THE meal was a rather quiet affair after that, mainly because Natalia had put herself on guard against Giancarlo Cardinale's irresistible charisma. But the food was surprisingly light and pleasant, which made her realise that he'd had more control over his Sicilian friend than he'd led her to believe.

He also controlled the small bouts of conversation they slid into, with what she read as his deliberate intention to keep the atmosphere light between them while they ate. So he talked, she listened, offered up a reply when it was absolutely necessary and in general tried very hard not to let herself become more fascinated with him than she was already.

But it was difficult when the man himself was a fascination even without his smooth, quiet, deeply sensual voice washing over her like a hypnotist's drone aimed to keep her trance-like.

Her eyes rarely left him so they missed very little: the way he lounged in his seat, the way he ate sparingly, the way he sipped at the half-bottle of crisp dry white wine he had ordered to suit his palate rather than the water...

'Are you sure you wouldn't like to try some?' he offered, tipping the bottle of wine towards her invitingly.

Natalia shook her head. They had reached the point in the meal where she was sitting over her empty plate with her elbows resting on the table and her glass suspended close to her mouth between her fingers. Her eyes had darkened, though she wasn't aware of it, and there was a softer

58

look about her which to him made her seem not of this world again.

Young, lovely, most definitely sexy, yet she gave off a conflicting aura of innocence. That aura bothered him, because it only helped to prove how good she was at projecting herself as something she wasn't.

Like most seasoned liars, he grimly concluded.

'A sip of white wine isn't going to compromise your ability to function efficiently, you know,' he heard himself snap in irritation.

Irritation at whom? he then asked himself. Her for being what she was or himself for wanting what she was?

'I'll fall asleep,' she said, offering a light shrug of her narrow shoulders when he flicked a sceptical glance at her. 'It happens,' she insisted. 'So I've learned to be careful.'

'You were drinking champagne at lunch yesterday,' he reminded her. 'And I don't recall you falling asleep afterwards.' In fact she was too feisty if anything, he added silently.

'Sipping sparingly at it,' she corrected. 'As I suspect everyone else was doing.'

'Apart from the rather impassioned young man you were with, who seemed to be downing it rather—feverishly.'

'Each to his own.' She shrugged again, refusing to take the bait he was offering her.

He smiled. He watched her watch the smile materialise with the kind of concentration that set his juices flowing. 'He fancied you like hell,' he inserted softly. 'And had to gulp champagne to stop himself making a grab for you.'

Her blue eyes began to flash a warning of anger. 'If you noticed that, then you should also have noticed that I didn't take him on,' she pointed out.

'With a face and a figure like yours, Miss Deyton,' he

derided, 'you should never need to take any man on because they will do all the running for you.'

'With cynicism like yours, Mr Cardinale,' she countered, 'I am not surprised that you hold that opinion.'

'Giancarlo,' he said, making those amazing eyes blink. 'My close friends call me Giancarlo...'

He sat back to watch lazily the way her spine began to straighten and the glass came carefully down upon the table—most effective body language, he determined.

'I'm an employee, not a friend,' she asserted, glancing pointedly at her gold wrist-watch as she did so.

She was preparing to back off again. He took his chance and snaked his hand out to capture one of hers as it began to slide away from the glass. Like a butterfly struggling in his palm, he felt her fingers flutter, then go perfectly still.

'You will call me Giancarlo from now on,' he repeated. 'And I will call you Natalia—you understand me?'

Yes, he saw that she understood very well what he was saying, but he also saw by the guard she'd placed on her eyes that she was never going to admit that. So he explained it more fully. 'I don't mind doing all the running when I am interested. In fact I rather enjoy it,' he admitted. 'But I mean to catch. So be prepared, *mia cara*,' he warned with smooth, sensual emphasis, 'for the time when *I* drink champagne with you. For it will not be to drown out my desires, but to inflame them. And you will drink and be inflamed also.'

Her cheeks were growing warm, her eyes darker. He watched her lean towards him over the table, and waited to see what she was going to come back with.

'It is not going to happen, *signor*, so forget it,' she said in hot rejection. Then she snatched her hand away and rose to her feet and, without another word, simply walked away from him.

*   *   *

He let her do it too! Natalia could feel him sitting there, burning mocking darts into her back as she wove her taut body between the restaurant tables on her way to the door.

Outside she paused for a moment to suck in some deep breaths of cold February air. Her cheeks were burning but her flesh felt like ice. And why not when she hadn't even got a coat on? The way she was shivering had nothing to do with him and what he'd dared to say to her! she told herself crossly.

But she had to get away from here, she decided, taking a few jerky steps before she pulled to a stop again. No coat, she repeated. No purse either. When he'd hurried her out into the taxi to come here, she hadn't given a thought to her personal items all still waiting where she had left them, in her fifth-floor office, which had been such a haven to her for the last six months—until Giancarlo Cardinale had decided to invade it!

Or invade her, she then amended with a squeezing sensation deep down in her body. An arm looped around her waist. She almost groaned in frustration. He stood at least six inches above her and was crowding her like a great grizzly bear!

Only he was no bear—grizzly or otherwise. He was smooth and sleek and tormentingly masculine. 'I don't want you to want me,' she told him in a thin, tight little voice.

'Too late,' he said. 'I already want you. All we need to do now is get you to admit that you want what I want, then we can place this affair on an even footing.'

'I don't have affairs,' she threw back. And *affair* just about said it for Natalia. Not relationship or even emotional involvement, but an affair of the body. Physical, basic.

She thought she heard him huff out a sound of scorn,

though she could have been mistaken because he was hailing down a passing black cab at the time. But even the suggestion that he was scorning her statement was enough to keep her tense and distant as he hustled her into the taxi.

Long, lean, and as lithe as hell, he sat down beside her, then proceeded to stretch his body so he could fish in his pocket for something while her body went into tension overload as she watched him, and the cabby waited for him to say where they were heading for next.

A piece of paper appeared. She recognised it as the same one he had been scrawling something down upon after his girlfriend had telephoned this morning.

If he's intending to take me to meet her, she thought hysterically, then he really is as crazy as I'm beginning to suspect!

He relayed an address on the other side of the City, then settled back beside her while the driver began feeding the cab into the traffic.

'I would prefer to go straight back to the office,' she told him frostily.

'We will, later,' he replied. 'We have things to do first...'

Which instantly shot her to pieces. 'I don't want to *do* anything with you!'

He looked at her, she looked at him, lightning flashed—and they fell on each other. It was that quick, that hot, and that torrid. Mouth straining against mouth, breathing fast and fevered. It was shocking, a terrible dive into absolute abandonment...

Giancarlo couldn't believe this was actually him! But he wanted her—badly—and he wanted her now! And it had to happen in the back of a London black cab, of all places, with no privacy and no hope of taking it where he desperately needed it to go!

But her mouth really did taste of heaven, as his senses had been telling him it would from the first moment he'd set eyes on her. The sheer exquisite I-can't-get-enough-of-this pleasure of it was completely taking him over. And while he devoured she let herself be eaten, denying him nothing—nothing.

She was his for the taking...

This shouldn't be happening, Natalia was telling herself over and over. It made no difference. She loved the taste of him too much, the tight masculine domination with which the kiss was being sold.

He tasted of wine, and hot desire. She was dizzy on one and burning up on the other.

Oh, someone save me! She groaned when his hand came to curve over one of her breasts and the flesh beneath came alive in a burgeoning thrust that must have left him in no doubt as to what she was feeling.

This was it, the point of no return for her. She knew it and she suspected that he knew it. She either stopped him now or she surrendered completely.

It was the taxi pulling to an abrupt standstill that had them both breaking apart. They had arrived, apparently, though Natalia was too dazed to know where they were.

To give him his due, if the cabby had noticed what they'd been doing in the back of his cab he made no sign of it as Giancarlo paid him, adding a rather large tip, she suspected, going by the pleasant way the driver responded.

Opening the door, Giancarlo reached for her hand, then stepped out on the pavement trailing her with him as he went. Neither had looked directly at the other since the

kiss. But she could feel its heat on her lips still and the
hand he had folded round one of hers was very possessive.

He was gazing at the frontage to a large building built
in stone which reminded her of just one of many Victorian
office blocks that dotted this area of the City. But when
they stepped into its luxurious foyer, she began to realise
that this was no ordinary office block, but a block of highly
exclusive City apartments, with a concierge who rose to
his feet behind his workstation and smiled politely as they
approached him.

Giancarlo gave his name and was handed a plastic card,
then was directed towards the lifts and told to use it in the
lift to gain access to the top floor. Natalia managed to take
back her hand as they walked towards the lift. He said
nothing. They still hadn't looked at each other.

No surprise there, she thought tensely, when you think
what happened the last time.

The lift doors slid open, and Giancarlo waited politely
for her to precede him inside. It was lined from ceiling to
floor with tinted mirror glass, and she went to stand in the
far corner and kept her face lowered because she just
didn't want to see what her reflection was going to tell her
if she did dare look up and catch a glimpse of herself. The
lift began to rise. Giancarlo had taken up a position in the
other corner across from her. She sensed his brooding
study but refused to meet it. The silence was stifling, the
tension so fraught it began lifting the hairs all over her
body. If something didn't break it soon she had a horrible
feeling she was going to burst out crying.

Maybe he knew it. 'Natalia,' he murmured, using her
name with husky intimacy that ran through her blood like
mercury. 'You can look at me; I am in control now.'

Well, bully for you, she thought with acid satire. Now
ask me if *I* am in control! But despite the inner quip, she

found herself lifting her head with a defiance that burned in her eyes as they hit him.

'Who owns this place?' she asked, using the first non-provoking question to pop into her head.

'A—friend of mine,' he answered with his voice—while his eyes most definitely brooded on other things. 'He is into property development. This building has only recently begun letting its space.'

'*Office* space?' she sliced sweetly at him.

'No.' He shook his dark head—and her fingers itched to grab hold of it and pull it down until his mouth hit hers. Oh, damn, she cursed…

Damn it… Giancarlo was cursing silently. If she continued to look at him like that it was likely he would stop this lift and show her how much it was costing him to remain this passive.

'Apartments,' he answered levelly. 'I need a place to stay while I am in London as well as a place to work from, and this will be the ideal solution.'

'You've been here before? Last night, for instance?'

Ah! He began to get an idea as to what was really eating at her. Not the serious risk of torrid sex in a rising lift—but the risk that she was about to be walked into his busy den of iniquity.

He allowed himself a small grimace, seeing that the hook he had used to concentrate her mind on him had now become a hindrance to the developing situation.

So, 'No,' he replied. 'Last night I stayed with the property developer himself and his lovely wife—Serena Delucca,' he placed succinctly, watching carefully as her expression began to show the slow dawning of full understanding.

'Playing games, *signor*?' she grimly mocked him.

'Don't we all, *signorina*?' he dryly returned.

Her breasts began to ache. They had no right to do so when the conversation could not be even vaguely considered sexual.

No? a little voice inside her head scoffed. Every single thing the two of you do or say is so sexual it should be X-rated!

The lift stopped. They both straightened away from the walls. The doors slid open. They stepped out together into a wide, light, square inner foyer with shiny white-tiled flooring and magnolia walls, and no doors but wide, deep-set, angular openings that linked room to room in a way meant to convey the impression of space and light and freedom of movement.

It also came pre-furnished, in a style designed to complement its open planning. Nothing stood out, nothing glared back at you, just a clever blend of natural shades and fabrics that were so easy on the eye you could almost miss them.

'Nice,' she said, not sure if she liked it.

'Bland,' he replied, showing he felt the same as she did. 'Serena's choice, if I am not mistaken. Being a black-haired, black-eyed witch, she likes to make an impression in any given situation. And she would make an impression in here,' he said.

Then he turned to look at Natalia.

'No,' she gasped when she saw his expression. But it was already too late. His hand snaked up, pulled the clasp from her hair, then stood back to watch the silken strands tumble in a glistening copper flow down her neck and over her shoulders until they settled like a caress to the curve of her breasts.

'Now that,' he drawled, 'is what I call making an impression.'

Copper-fire hair, white skin, rose-coloured lips, wide, shock-darkened lover-blue eyes, he listed covetously. Long black suit hugging a slender body, breasts that wanted to feel his touch again—and a pair of amazing legs which were taking her backwards in a useless bid for escape.

She'd missed her only chance, he saw, as her wary reversing took her right away from the open lift. Which left her with nowhere else to go but deeper into the apartment, treading bright white tiles on slender heels that made tiny tapping sounds as she went.

He began to track her, his hand snaking out to flick the button that would send the lift away. Watching him do it, she realised her mistake, her lips fell open and began to tremor, and his chest began to beat to the drum of the chase.

'Th-this isn't funny,' she stammered on a constricted flow of air.

'I am not laughing,' he pointed out, lifting his hand up to the knot of his tie to slowly begin pulling at it.

If it was possible her eyes grew wider, flickering from his fingers to his eyes in a slightly wild stare of disbelief.

He said nothing else. He didn't need to. The tie came loose and he began sliding it leisurely from around his throat. He let it fall in a snake-like slither to the floor, then began unhooking shirt buttons.

She went stock-still—then jerked a hand up to press it against her upper chest, and he smiled as he came to a standstill, because he knew she had picked up the same beat he was feeling.

'Going to stop me?' he taunted softly while his fingers

continued slowly slipping open buttons. 'All you need to do is say the word, and it stops right here...'

The big test. The acid test. Natalia knew she was hovering on the edge of a rather large precipice. She either backed herself right off it, or she held her ground. It was her choice. He was giving her the choice.

Her mouth was dry, her throat tight, her body pulsing to its own hectic rhythm. There he was, standing there, no longer looking quite so razor-sharp any more, with his tie gone and his shirt buttons half open down his front so she could see tantalising glimpses of golden skin and dark body hair—and even smell that illusive scent she recognised on an another level of consciousness as utterly seductive.

Pheromone, they called it. The sexually aroused male putting out messages to the sexually aware female.

But *this* male and *this* female—? She lifted her gaze to his dark, compelling eyes and saw the capital red letters DANGER gleaming warningly there. Think of the complications, she told herself. Think of Edward—the lies! Think what you could be risking here!

Think of that mouth fixed on your mouth, her foolish heart suggested, sending her eyes flickering again on a downward path over a face she didn't seem to be able to look at enough. Then onto his hands, which made her flesh tingle with excitement, and his body, which filled her with such clamouring hunger.

And what was it but sex? she tried telling herself. I can do that! I can live with that! I can enjoy this man then let him go when it's time to call a stop to it before it has a chance to hurt other people! I can do it, she insisted, and felt her heart give a heavy thump at the decision, then start racing furiously as if it knew something she didn't...

What was she thinking? What was going on inside that beautiful head to make her stand there looking at him like that? Indecision? Uncertainty?

Loyal thoughts of Edward?

The very suggestion made something violent wrench inside of him, and in angry response to it he began striding forward. He didn't want to hear Edward's name falling from her trembling lips, so he was going to make damn sure it didn't happen!

Reaching for her, he fed his fingers into her glorious mass of hair, used his thumbs to cup her chin so he could keep that exquisite face turned up to his—then lowered his head and kissed her. The sheer heat of her response reached right down to the very core of his manhood. He heard himself groan. She let out a little whimper that told him she was experiencing exactly the same as he. The knowledge soared like a phoenix rising out of the fire of his anger to consume him with the need to make her catch fire too.

He altered his stance, inviting her closer. She came without hesitation, sinking into him and lifting her hands to fold them around his neck while he sent his sliding slowly downwards. Over her shoulders, down her back, feeling the hectic pulse of her heart as he passed over her ribcage, then on down until finally they settled against the curving firmness of her hips.

And through it all their mouths strained against each other. Warm and hungry, soft and deep. He was back in control. The seduction was on. They had only one place to go from here.

Yet—what did he do?

He broke the kiss, looked deep into her passion-glazed, most definitely sultry blue eyes which held all the promises of life's rarest pleasures just waiting for him to tap into them—and he changed his mind.

'No,' he said, quietly and very calmly.

She began to frown, her softly parted, gently pulsing mouth still feeling his mouth against it. 'No?' she replied in sweet confusion.

'No,' he confirmed, but kissed her again to soften the blow before he added huskily, 'We will not do this now. The timing is bad. We have an apartment to view. I have an important meeting to attend in less than an hour. I should be ashamed of myself. You deserve better than a quick roll on the nearest bed we can find. I beg your forgiveness. Next time I will show a little more—finesse, I promise you.'

'Finesse,' she repeated, seeming to register only that one word out of everything he had said. Her eyelashes fluttered down, making the tip of his tongue tingle with a desire to reach out and follow their gently curving spread against her cheekbones. Her body drew back, her fingers trailing very slowly from his nape to his chest, where his gaping shirt proved no barrier against the burning touch of her palms as she flatted them against him—then pushed him away.

He had hurt her, he could see it. She felt humiliated and cheap. But he couldn't change the unpalatable fact that having suspected that she was thinking of Edward just when he'd kissed her had effectively ruined what had been promising to be a mind-blowing experience for him.

Because no woman, he vowed with an inner harshness that narrowed his eyes when she flicked up those lashes to look at him again—no woman thinks of another man when she should be thinking of Giancarlo Cardinale! In fact, the next time he brought Natalia Deyton to a point of complete surrender, he would make absolutely certain that she did no thinking at all!

So, 'Unless, of course, you prefer the quick roll?' he offered with just enough of a taunt in his tone to make her eyes flash.

'Why?' she came back like the flick of a whip. 'Is that all that's on offer?'

Oh, very good... He began to grin. The English had a saying for this, he mused, something to do with being foisted or hoisted on one's own petard. He began to laugh. He was enjoying himself again.

While she looked ready to attack him like a deranged cat.

Well, that was okay. He could deal with that. In fact, he would look forward to it. Only this particular cat would be purring for him by the time the deed was done...

I'll swing for him. I promise I will! Natalia vowed as she turned and walked stiffly away. When she'd managed to calm down a little she would begin to appreciate what a lucky escape she'd had!

For the man was a tease—an arrogant tease. He ought to know better at his age. Unless, of course, leading women on then backing off once he had them where he wanted them was the way Giancarlo Cardinale got his sexual kicks!

And she had surrendered. That telling little truth shuddered through her on a shaft of self-disgust as she stepped through the first opening that she came to—then stopped dead in utter surprise at what her eyes were being treated to.

Because she had never seen anything quite like it. The room—if you could call it a room—opened out into a square-shaped arena with a high white ceiling and a polished maple floor, which went down in steps to a sunken seating area furnished with soft cream leather sofas and chairs. In its centre sat a slab of marble that was supposed to be a table, she assumed. And the walls were painted in the palest yellow, the long plain hung curtains of lined white voile.

'I think we have found the sitting room,' a sardonic voice murmured behind her.

She would have stiffened in revolt, but she was just too overcome by what she was seeing. 'You're really going to live here?' she asked, unable to imagine anyone actually using this place!

'Looks like it,' he answered, stepping past her to walk down into the seating area, where he shoved his hands into his trouser pockets and began to look around.

He'd done up his shirt, Natalia noted. In the short walk from where she had left him to him joining her here, he had tidied away all the evidence of his little after-lunch diversion. Even his tie was back around his neck, though hanging loose there, at least.

'Come down here and take a look at this,' he said, unaware of the bitter thoughts going through her head.

She went because it was easier to do that than argue. 'Some bachelor pad,' he drawled, nodding towards one of the walls where another doorless opening led straight into a bedroom. You could even see the bed—a vast low-slung thing covered in snowy white linen. 'I even have the sacrificial altar on which to lay out my victims.'

He was amused, but as she looked at the slab of marble posing as a table through a new set of eyes she felt herself blushing like an idiot.

'Not yet,' he whispered close to her ear, sending her nerve-ends screaming for cover.

But before she could retaliate with something really cutting, he was frowning at his watch and already turning away. 'We are running out of time,' he clipped out as if the other provocative remark had never been uttered. 'Let's see the rest of the place. We need to find somewhere to set up operations before a team of technicians arrive to connect us up.'

The idea of having to work here with him on a daily basis was becoming less palatable by the minute. But she followed him through room after room of minimalism gone mad. The dining room, for instance, almost matched the living room in style and texture. The kitchen was more white floor tiling, more maple wood, with more marble and some stainless steel thrown in as a feature.

As he'd said. The perfect bachelor pad.

There was even a room set up ready as a designer office. 'Ah,' Giancarlo said, glancing round them. 'At last I begin to see why Fredo suggested this place.'

So could she. Thinking of it from a strictly business point of view—and she was determined to keep her view of this situation *strictly* business from now on—this was absolutely ideal for what she assumed was required of the busy venture capitalist wanting to work from home.

All it lacked at the moment was its communications hardware to link him into anywhere he wanted to go. The rest was already provided for. The workstations, the chairs—even the sunlight he professed to need for his Sicilian blood to run smoothly through his veins was managing to filter in through the voile-covered window.

It was her own needs which were beginning to trouble her because there was no separate office for her to escape to for a bit of relief from his relentless personality.

Also, it was right on the other side of town from Knight's—and her own home in Chelsea.

'What's the matter?' As sharp as a needle, he picked up on her concern.

'Nothing,' she said, turning away from him, suddenly feeling so weary she just wanted to sit down in a dark corner somewhere and sulk. 'How soon do you intend to move in here?' she asked, looking for a diversion, and finding it where she did not want it to be.

'Now,' he announced. 'We will do it now. I will make a few phone calls to get things started, then leave you here to oversee the installation of everything we require while I shoot off to Knight's to meet with my staff.'

'But I need to go back there myself!' she protested. 'I've left my things there—my coat, my purse, my—'

'No problem. I will collect anything of yours and bring it with me when I return,' he insisted, not even seeming to see her look of angry dismay at the way he was completely taking her over like this! 'By the time I get back, I expect this place to be up and running,' he warned, already lifting a mobile phone from his pocket and punching in numbers while Natalia sank into the nearest chair in an air of defeat.

It was like being in the presence of a human dynamo and she just didn't have any energy left with which to keep up with him. So she didn't bother—the chair was as good as any dark corner to sulk in at this precise moment. So she sat there and simply let his voice waft over her head as he made call after call and she pondered the miseries of crossing London on a daily basis just to endure more of—this.

'Okay. Everything is organised,' he said eventually. 'The technicians will be here in half an hour. They know what I want. Make sure that everything is up and running before you let them leave.' He glanced at his watch, frowned and began heading for the door that wasn't a door.

'Give the concierge a call,' he instructed over his shoulder. 'Find out the name of the nearest supermarket and get some provisions delivered here. I will be back—whenever.' He was already at the lift. 'Until then—make yourself at home...'

CHAPTER FIVE

MAKE yourself at home…

Well, Natalia decided to do just that. Giancarlo wanted provisions? He got provisions. He wanted his office up and running by the time he got back? He got his office up and running by the time he got back. He even got the office drawers and cupboards stocked with every miscellaneous item known to the nearest office stores suppliers she could locate as soon as the telephone line was connected.

Efficiency was her middle name, she decided. No one could fault her organisation skills! Everything was neatly filed, everything had its own neatly printed tab. In fact, in the few hours she'd had, she'd brought Signor Cardinale's nice new workplace to life with an absolute vengeance.

And vengeance felt like a very good word to her at this precise moment while she sat in her chosen chair at her chosen monitor screen, in her chosen corner of the room, doing exactly what she was paid to do, which was dealing with all the neglected business of the day that had arrived in her network-linked work-folder while she had been otherwise engaged.

In fact she was just finishing up when the sound of the lift drawing to a halt alerted her to his return, so even her timing was super-efficient, she made a very satisfied note, glancing at her watch as she did so.

Seven o'clock, it told her. Which made her a very dedicated personal assistant with super-efficient secretarial skills! she mocked herself grimly as she shut down her network-link to Knight's.

Outside it had been dark for hours, so it was a long time since she'd gone round the apartment switching on lights and drawing curtains. But although the place had taken on a more appealing image with the subtle use of artificial lighting, she was heartily glad to be getting out of it.

She stood up as she heard his footsteps sound in the white-tiled foyer. By the time he appeared in the opening she had stepped around her chair and was just unhooking her suit jacket from its backrest. Glancing up, she found herself looking into a lean dark face that was beginning to look a little jaded round the edges. He needed a shave, his shirt was open at the neck again, the tie knotted but hanging loose as if tugged like that by impatient fingers. Over his arm lay her coat, her soft lilac scarf, and he was holding a plastic carrier bag in which, she presumed, was her handbag.

The desire to voice a polite greeting to him was not even an option. She was angry, and if it weren't for her loyalty to Edward she would have walked out of this apartment hours ago, gone to collect her own things from Knight's, then walked out of there too, with the intention of never returning!

But as things stood regarding her commitment to Edward, she merely demonstrated her anger with Ginacarlo Cardinale by flicking her eyes away from him, then completely ignoring him as she finished pulling on her jacket.

But that did not mean she wasn't hotly aware that his eyes were sliding over the dark red top she was in the process of covering up...

Red on red, he was thinking, wanting to voice some deep, dark, sensual question as to why the red of her wonderful hair was not clashing with the red of her very sexy top.

But he was too alive to the silent warning that any comment at all from him was not going to be appreciated.

She was back behind her frosty wall, he made note, then grimaced because—hell, who could blame her? Separated, isolated, and infiltrated were the buzzwords which came to mind to describe what he had done to Natalia Deyton.

Then he'd left her alone here to stew on it all for hours upon end with the deliberate intention of keeping her balanced on an emotional edge, ready to tip over whenever he felt like making it happen.

So, no wonder she looked frosty. No wonder her chin was up and her mouth pulled into that flat little line of stiff disapproval meant to convey a warning to him that if he said just one word out of place she would most probably kill him.

But, *Dio*, she looked sensational in her anger with her hair streaming down her back like a proud defiance in her absolute refusal to redress what he had arrogantly undressed earlier.

'Your luggage has arrived.' She spoke suddenly.

His loins gave him a vicious kick because that icy voice was just begging to be melted.

'I had it placed in your room for you to deal with.'

Her fingers were busy fastening buttons on the severe black jacket that did nothing to hide the body beneath and, even if it had, he would still have been able to feel the firmness of her breast against his palm so it wouldn't have mattered anyway.

'Also, a car was delivered.' She pointed to a set of keys lying on the workstation set up near the window. 'You will find it parked down in the basement. Black, I believe,' she added with just the merest hint of acid. 'Of the Italian variety. Not easy to miss, I should think...'

And that, he read, had been a deliberate strike at his

masculine ego for his choice of car in a traffic-blocked city like London. She would have been more impressed by a small nondescript run-about than his brand new phallic-symbol Ferrari, he judged, and almost sent her a provocative challenging smile—but the conditions didn't advise it.

Because, despite all the frosty defiance, she looked tired and a little pale and the finest hint of bruising was beginning to darken the sockets of her beautiful eyes. Oddly, he didn't like to see it. For all he was aware that his siege tactics were a deliberate part of his divide and conquer war of attrition, he had no wish to lay to waste that part of her which had fired his motives in the first place.

So he did absolutely nothing as he watched her turn to walk towards him with her jacket buttoned up to her stiff neck, and her eyes as cold as the Arctic. Coming to a stop in front of him, she reached out to take her scarf first, sliding it off his arm and looping it around her neck before reaching for her coat. He said not a thing as the warm cashmere-wool mix settled across her shoulders, its long length reaching way beyond her slender calves. Nor remarked when, with a careless grace, she slid the long pelt of her hair out from inside the coat, then reached out to take the carrier bag containing her handbag.

'Goodnight,' she said, and walked proudly away from him.

It really was a sensational performance. Shame it was all spoiled by the distinct threat of tears he had glimpsed in her eyes just before she'd turned away...

Nothing, she was telling herself as she walked. No words, no expression, no attempt to thank her for the hours she had put in here for his benefit—not even a hint that he was aware of everything else he had put her through today! She hated him, she really did!

But what really hurt was that he'd let her walk away just now. Why should it hurt? she asked herself as she stabbed an angry finger at the lift-call button. What was the matter with her? Was she an absolute sucker for punishment or something? The man was cruel, he played cruel games like a cat would with a mouse before it gobbled its victim up and spit out the bones. Was that what Giancarlo Cardinale had in store for her? A final gobbling up of her before he spit out what was left and walked away?

'Oh, come on—come on!' she begged the lift, feeling the tears begin to threaten for real now.

She went to hit the button again—found her fingers clashing with another set of fingers and glanced up to see through a veil of tears—him standing beside her.

Her hand snapped away. 'Forgotten something?' she asked, meaning to sound sarcastic, but she only managed husky and wished she weren't such an emotional fool.

'No,' he replied, quietly, levelly. 'It was you who forgot me.'

The lift arrived. She frowned, not understanding his meaning. Then decided she didn't *want* to understand it as she stepped into the lift and turned to press for the ground-floor foyer—when once again his hand beat her to it.

He pressed for the basement. 'I am driving you home,' he explained.

Standing there, not half an inch separating her from his whipcord lean, muscle-hardened, *arrogant* stance, she noticed the bunch of car keys dangling from his lean dark fingers, looked up at his carefully neutral expression, and said, 'Go to hell,' thickly, succinctly. Then reached out *again* to press for the ground-floor foyer, and had her hand firmly captured, stopping her from touching anything—but him.

Sensation hit her in a crackling rush that fled round her system. She tried to break free, got herself pinned for her trouble against mirror-lined walls that sent back reflected images of the two of them from just about every angle. It was mad, compelling. Dark face—white face. Black hair—copper hair. Flashing blue eyes—steady brown velvet. And two mouths coming closer as if unable to resist the hypnotic pull of the other.

'Don't...' she whispered in a last-ditch attempt to save herself from disaster.

He drew back. She hated him for it. 'Do you allow me to drive you home,' he levelled quietly, 'or do we return upstairs to—discuss the matter?'

What a choice. The ultimate ultimatum, she recognised, for, despite his level voice, the quiet, calm manner, she knew what was being put on offer here. Escape, the chance to live another day—or capture, in its most consummate sense.

The silence sizzled with hesitation. It ate at her senses and burned in her breasts. His hands were locked on her upper arms, hers were flattened against his rock-solid chest, so she could feel the steady pound of his heart, and the even spacing of his breath. But she could also feel her own heart rattling around as if in a whirlpool—panicking because she wasn't breathing at all.

The decision was that difficult to make...

If she chose to go back upstairs, he would be the loser here, Giancarlo told himself, because she would be coming to his bed still fighting him, and by tomorrow she would hate him for it.

But he didn't want her hatred. He wanted her warm and

willing and believing that to be with him in his bed was the only place she wanted to be. In fact, it was essential she feel like that. For what good was a single night of passion going to do him when it came to seducing her right away from Edward?

It was the long-term seduction of Natalia Deyton which was the real goal he had set himself—making her want him enough and trust him enough to need him more than she'd ever needed anyone.

But if she chose to go home, he wasn't sure he could let her go that easily either. She had no idea what her eyes were telling him, he thought tensely. No suspicion that he was being eaten up inside. She was tying him in knots, he freely admitted it. Sensual knots, emotional knots. Greedy, compulsive, frustrated knots that made a complete mockery of the offer to drive her home.

He'd meant to be kind, show her another side to himself that was thoughtful and caring because she'd looked so tired and stressed out. He'd discovered he didn't like it—didn't like knowing that her strain was entirely his fault.

'I need to go home,' she whispered throatily. And the tears were still there! He wanted to kick himself for making them happen. He wanted to say to hell with it all and simply take her back to his apartment anyway!

They came to a stop and the doors slid open, revealing two fellow tenants waiting to enter, their polite expressions trying hard not to notice the buzz of sexual tension bouncing off the mirrored walls of the lift-car.

Giancarlo straightened away from her instantly. Natalia quickly slid herself past both him and the two others with her head lowered so they couldn't see her pained embarrassment.

He joined her as the lift doors closed again, leaving them

alone in the softly lit car park with a double row of expensive cars.

The Ferrari still stood out as different, squatting low and sleek in its reserved slot, like a black cat waiting to pounce the moment it was given the opportunity.

Deactivating its state-of-the-art security, he walked round to the passenger door and opened it for her. She didn't say a single word but just folded herself into the plush leather seat and waited for him to close the door.

She was staring directly ahead when he climbed in beside her. He adjusted the seat to accommodate his long legs, clipped home his seat belt, and then fired the engine. The car had been parked front end out so all he had to do was put it in gear and they were moving with a low purring growl that made his teeth clench with pleasure because, no matter what Natalia felt about this car, he was Italian, and his Italian blood revelled in that sound like no other.

Except the purr of a woman, he ruefully considered. Then he shut down that line of thinking before it took him places he couldn't afford to go right now...

Outside in the street it had started raining. Natalia sat watching heavy sheets of the stuff slating down from a leaden sky, and knew she would have been soaked through to the skin before she'd walked ten feet in this kind of downpour.

Which made rather a mockery out of her stiff-faced bid for independence earlier, she acknowledged. Doing it her own way, she would have arrived home looking like a drowned rat and feeling more miserable than she already did!

'Where to?' he asked.

'Chelsea,' she told him shortly. Then, because she was beginning to feel the unfair sting of her own churlish manner, especially when she remembered that he had arrived at his apartment looking tired, yet here he was, driving her home in weather not fit for dogs, she lightened her tone to add, 'It's on the other side of the river. If you—'

'I know where Chelsea is,' he cut in levelly.

She floundered into silence again, realising she should have remembered that he was quite familiar with London. Edward had told her once that Giancarlo had worked here in the City for a few years when he'd been just beginning to strike out on his own 'playing the hot-shot City broker and cutting quite a dash with the ladies,' Edward had fondly described the Giancarlo of those days. But then, Edward was deeply fond of his wife's younger brother, she recalled heavily. Which made this other situation that was so quickly developing all the more impossible.

Oh, Edward, she thought sighingly. What am I going to do? What *am* I going to do—?

No answer came back because Edward wasn't here, but she was and so was Giancarlo, driving together, through a rainy London evening in a car that turned heads even in this kind of weather—and with an atmosphere inside the car that sang with sexual tension, even though they were both trying to pretend it wasn't there.

She began feeding him directions once they were nearing their destination, her voice sounding huskily intimate, even to her. The rain stopped quite suddenly as they turned into her street. She directed him to a parking spot by the kerb outside her house and inside she was beginning to tremble slightly as the car stopped and the engine died.

For it was, she realised, the beginning of yet another dangerous situation: the point where she said a polite thank-you and goodnight—or invited him inside.

'Nice house,' he commented, pre-empting her need to say anything. He was peering out of the car at the row of tiny cottages. 'It must cost you something to live here,' opined the astute banker in him. 'How many of you share, to rent a place like this?'

Casually said, merely curious more than anything, but still Natalia felt herself stiffening as a hint of warning went chasing down her spine. 'I don't rent,' she answered warily. 'And I don't share...'

She doesn't rent, and she doesn't share, Giancarlo was slowly repeating to himself, and suddenly felt himself going cold. He wasn't a fool, he knew the price of property in London, especially in a fashionable area like this. So how did a young woman trained as nothing more than a secretary, earning the salary he knew Natalia Deyton earned, afford to live here?

The answer came back like a stab in the chest. She couldn't afford it—but Edward could.

He was sitting here with another man's mistress, staring at another man's love-nest! And for a terrible moment he thought he was going to be sick!

Edward in there, with Natalia. Edward in there, cheating on his wife—cheating on Giancarlo's sister—with Natalia! His eyes began to burn into the brick frontage as if he could see every salacious thing they did in there.

'M-my mother passed away about fourteen months ago, if you recall,' Natalia was telling him huskily.

His black eyes flashed to her profile on a flare of hope. 'And you lived here together before she died?'

She went pale. 'I...n-no.'

The answer gutted him.

'Sh-she left me well provided for,' the little liar embroidered her tale of deceit. 'I just prefer to live alone. W-would you like to come in, h-have some coffee before you start back?' she offered—as a diversion tactic perhaps, to stop him probing any deeper into her financial arrangements?

Well, no, he would not like to come in! They would not carry him dead over the threshold of that—den of sin! he thought through the roaring in his ears. 'It is late,' he refused, amazed at how even his voice sounded. 'And it has been a long day. I think we are both tired...'

She looked so relieved that he had to presume she'd been terrified of him walking in there and discovering some little piece of evidence that would lead him to Edward.

'Then I'll say thank you, for bringing me home.' She didn't push the issue, found a brief smile—and was reaching for the door catch when he stopped her.

'Have dinner with me,' he said gruffly. 'Tomorrow night.'

She turned a puzzled frown on him. He didn't blame her—he was confused himself! All he knew was that things had changed. He wanted her out of that house and in his bed in *his* apartment before another day went by!

'I will be out all day tomorrow,' he went on, thinking on his feet again. 'I have meetings to attend in the City, so I won't see you unless you wait for me to get in tomorrow. So I am asking you to have dinner with me,' he repeated.

'What—like a date?' she asked, looking into his eyes with her own so wide and seductively vulnerable, he hated himself for the blast of heat he felt where he shouldn't!

'Yes, a date,' he confirmed, gruffly and suggestively. 'One where we get to know each other outside the work environment, and explore the—possibilities to what we know is already here...' He touched her soft and crushable lower lip with a finger. The warm flesh pulsed in instant response. 'Bring a change of clothes with you tomorrow, change at the apartment to save us some time…' In a minute, he thought fiercely, she will be licking that finger, and *Dio*, but he was burning for her to do it! 'It will be good, hmm?'

She knew what he was saying, the sultry look in her deceitful eyes told him so, as did the sensual pulse in the air surrounding them. And as his body throbbed and his anger roared and his eyes burned with his intentions, he felt that softly pulsing lip move on her answer.

'Yes,' she said.

Triumph sang in his blood. After tomorrow night she would not be sleeping in Edward's cosy little love-nest ever again! She was his for the taking, and he was going to take her! By the time this thing was over Natalia Deyton was going to belong to *him* body and soul, Giancarlo vowed.

Body and wretched lying soul…

CHAPTER SIX

BY SEVEN-FIFTEEN the next evening, Natalia was standing in the bedroom of Giancarlo's apartment, hurriedly putting the finishing touches to her make-up before she found herself somewhere to go to wait for him that wasn't so—thought provoking.

She couldn't believe an apartment of this size and class had only one bedroom and bathroom in it! A bachelor pad, he had dryly described it. One with hardly any doors and no locks on the few that it did have!

He had not arrived yet, and her tummy was fluttering with a nervous anticipation that was making it impossible for her to put her lipstick on straight. Sighing, she grabbed a tissue to wipe it away, then tried again.

It had been a strange day all told, she reflected. Disturbingly quiet without him here, yet she'd been feeling his presence everywhere from the moment she'd stepped out of the lift this morning.

No, before that, she amended, recalling the private taxicab that had arrived at her front door early this morning, arranged by him, to transport her here with the minimum of fuss and the maximum of comfort. The man certainly knew how to make an impression, she mused dryly. First with the door-to-door transport, then with the concierge waiting in the foyer to hand her the necessary security access card so that she could activate the lift, and an apology from Mr Cardinale for not being here today. 'I am instructed to inform you that he will be here to collect you at seven-thirty...'

Seven-thirty had seemed a comfortingly long way off then—but the man himself hadn't. From the moment she'd stepped out of the lift she had felt him everywhere she went in the apartment. Here in the bedroom, for instance, where she'd come first to hang up the suit bag carrying her clothes for tonight. The first thing to hit her had been the clean-scented smell of his soap permeating out from the connecting bathroom. And the evidence of his occupation lay everywhere she happened to look, like the loose change on the bedside table and the black cotton robe tossed casually on the bed.

A bed she couldn't so much as glance at without feeling her skin prickle as her mind shot off to places it shouldn't.

'Oh, heck,' she cursed softly, and made herself finish the job she had started before her nerves completely got the better of her. It had been bad enough taking a quick shower in his bathroom, hurrying herself through the chore with her senses on edge, tautly aware of the lack of a lock on the door and listening out for the sound of him returning early, terrified he would catch her there naked yet wickedly turned on by the idea at the same time. In fact she'd shocked herself by how vivid that fantasy had been.

She ought to be ashamed of herself. The note he'd left her had invited her to feel free to use the apartment as her own—but it had not given her permission to weave fantasies about him in his shower!

But then, it had been a week for heightening the senses. Yesterday she had spent in a constant state of high anxiety not knowing what he was going to come at her with next. Today, even though he had been physically absent, he had hovered silently in the background of everything she'd done, like the warm breath of a prospective lover on her nape, making his desires felt.

Oh, stop it! she scolded herself and began feeding her

cosmetics back into their bag with impatient fingers. It was the sheer volume of work he'd left for her to do that made it feel he were breathing down her neck! she told herself crossly.

So much work, in fact, that she decided he must have stayed up all night to produce it! Letters to type. Memos to create and wing off to all the separate departments in Knight's, carefully spelling out his directives and what he expected back from each and every one. Then there was the pin number he had left her, to enable her access to the Cardinale Group computer mainframe. A long list of jobs regarding all his other business interests had given her a daunting insight into how powerful a man he actually was.

No wonder she had become so obsessed by his presence, she told herself. He'd even emailed her at precisely one o'clock, ordering her to stop and make herself some lunch!

Then, halfway through the afternoon, the package had arrived by special courier. Her fingers went still, her eyes flickering up to catch their darkened expression in the mirror as she replayed that moment when she'd been handed the glossy white garment box—with the Taylor-Gant name inscribed in gold on the lid—and instantly known what had been inside it.

'Consider these homework,' the accompanying note said, scrawled in his bold black mocking hand. 'I trust your good judgement as to which set you choose to wear tonight.'

Inside the box had been no less than three different sets of underwear. A sheer black lace set, a flimsy white silk set and a daring set in come-and-get-me red. All of which were so sensually provocative that she'd actually blushed as she'd visualised him choosing these things for her to wear!

But she was wearing the white set, which was telling her something she had no wish to dwell upon right now.

A telephone began to ring. Almost jumping out of her skin as the sound pierced the silence, she turned rather dazedly to look for the nearest extension line. She found it next to the bed, and went to answer it warily, knowing somehow that it had to be him.

'Did you carry out all my instructions?' his low, dark, huskily intimate voice murmured enquiringly, and made her instantly aware of delicate white silk lovingly moulding her body.

'I finished all the work you required me to do,' she replied coolly, refusing to take up the bait.

He laughed softly and the sound sent her legs weak.

'Where are you?' she asked, glancing down at her watch to see that it was exactly seven-thirty.

'Right here in the foyer,' he told her. 'Awaiting my date—are you coming down?'

Coming down? She frowned. 'Don't you need to change first?'

'Would you *like* me to come up?'

'No!' she cried, not understanding why she was being handed this reprieve from the one moment she had been dreading all day, but more than willing to accept it. 'I just need a few minutes and I will come down to you.'

Already beginning to panic, she put down the phone, then turned in an anxious daze to gather the last of her things together. She would have to collect them tomorrow, she told herself as she stuffed her day things into the suit bag with fingers that trembled in her urgency. For it wouldn't be practical for her to come back here tonight just to collect them.

Who needs a practical excuse to come back here? a little voice inside her head mocked.

Ignoring it, she turned to take a last quick glance at herself in the mirror. What she saw reflected back at her set her nerve-ends singing. Was that her—was it really her?

Her cheeks were flushed, her eyes were too bright—and the dress was an absolute disaster! It was too short, too tight, too—everything! she decided, giving a wriggling tug at the stretchy fabric in an effort to cover up some more leg. The dusky-blue silk-knit settled back to its original position the moment she let go of it—leaving her standing there staring at it in despair. She had deliberately chosen this particular dress because she'd thought it had all the right qualities to look elegant and demure with its long sleeves and what she'd remembered as a modest V neckline.

So how was it that she hadn't remembered how it clung to her body like a second skin? Or that the V dipped too low into her cleavage and her legs suddenly looked twice as long as they were!

And I should have put my hair up! she realised as panic put its foot on the throttle and went raging through her at full pace. Leaving it down to hang loose over her shoulders made her look—slinky, she saw in growing horror.

Had she time to stand here messing with it? The overriding fear of him losing patience and coming up here to find her told her she hadn't even got time to panic like this!

'Oh,' she groaned. This was all *his* fault! The wretched man had been slowly driving her out of her mind all day.

Then—no, she amended that as she shuffled her feet into three-inch high-heeled shoes and made a grab for her evening jacket. He had been driving her out of her mind from the first moment she'd set eyes on him two days ago!

Was it only two days? It felt like for ever, she thought

tensely as she snatched up her evening purse and left the bedroom.

She was hurrying past the kitchen opening when she spied the ice bucket sitting on one of the units with the bottle of champagne standing in it—and pulled to a stop, then closed her eyes on the unwanted reminder of this particular instruction he'd emailed her.

Five o'clock on the dot, she recalled with a tense little quiver. 'You may stop being the efficient Miss Deyton now and turn yourself into the very desirable Natalia for me. PS. Put the champagne on ice,' leaving her in no doubt as to his expectations later tonight.

But what really bothered her was—she'd done it. What did that tell her about her own expectations for tonight?

But—no. Grimly she blocked out that thought. They were going out for dinner, she told herself firmly as she stepped into the lift and pressed for the foyer. *Dinner,* she repeated. Nothing more, nothing less. When it was over she would go home to her own house and her own bed, and Giancarlo Cardinale would be drinking his champagne alone.

A promise she forgot the moment she set eyes on him. The lift doors came open as he was turning round to face them. She gained a very vague impression of subtle lighting and white tiled flooring, then—nothing.

He went still. So did she, the breath dying in her throat. He was wearing a dark suit, white shirt and a dark tie, all of which looked as if he had put them on only minutes ago. His face was clean-shaven, his hair as smooth as silk. He looked lean and dark and frighteningly special—and his eyes were so hot they made her flesh burn...

Had it worked? Giancarlo was asking himself tensely as he turned to watch the lift doors open. Had he managed to keep her mind so totally focused on him all day that she would not be able to think of any other man?

One look at her flushed, slightly guarded expression as the lift doors opened, and he had his answer.

Dio—yes! he exclaimed on a silent hiss of triumph that made his heart vibrate. She was his, those darkened eyes were seeing no other man but him, thinking of no other man—wanting no other man.

And this one wanted her with a craving that was threatening to take him over. She looked sensational. All fire and light and simmering senses, he expanded on a hot sense of masculine pleasure for the way those eyes were looking at him. Eyes that did things to him no other pair of eyes had ever done. The eyes, the hair, the wonderful skin, he listed. The body inside the sensually moulding fabric of her dress that brought vivid pictures to mind of what was going on unseen and did things to his libido that actually shocked him.

And then there was the mouth, he came to finally. It was a mouth to revel in, lose himself in, a mouth he had acquired a hungry taste for and intended to taste over and over again very soon.

In fact his driving impulse was to leap the gap between them and devour her right there and then in the lift on the way back upstairs. But there was also an overriding desire burning in him that simply wanted to enjoy watching her long legs bring her towards him.

His, all his, he claimed possessively. And stepped smoothly forward to gallantly take hold of her hand. *'Buona sera, signorina,'* he greeted softly. *'Non è bello quel che è bello, ma è bello quel che piace...'*

Somewhere in the background the concierge was watching all of this with smiling indulgence. Neither of them seemed to notice. Giancarlo was too engrossed in what was happening to her eyes again, and Natalia was trying to come to terms with the way his voice in its native Italian had affected her. She felt hot and stripped and touched all over!

'What did you say?' she asked, wary in case she was responding this violently to some bland remark about the time!

'Loosely translated?' he asked. 'Beauty is not for the one who is beautiful, but is beauty for the one who it pleases,' he huskily supplied.

She blushed; he smiled and caught her hand. 'You could reply here that I am good to look upon also,' he teasingly suggested.

But she shook her head. 'I'm not even going to try and compete with an Italian male speaking his own language,' she refused, then she smiled too, ruefully. 'You could have been telling me about the weather,' she confessed. 'It would still probably sound just as—sensual,' was the only word she could come up with.

The way his fingers moved around hers told her he'd liked her choice of word. 'Let me assure you, then,' he said, turning them towards the exit. 'No Italian male worth his salt would talk about the weather to a beautiful woman. It would be seen as a crime, believe me...'

Oh, she believed him all right. Didn't they say that the Italian male came out of the womb knowing the art of seduction?

'Where are we going?' She changed the subject. And tried not to notice how his body was brushing lightly against her own or inhale the same clean scent that had been tormenting her all day.

'Somewhere we will not be hovered over by an anxious compatriot,' he said with a dry clip to his tone as he pulled open one of the plate-glass doors and politely stepped back so that she could precede him through it.

He didn't relinquish her hand though. 'He was nice,' she defended the proprietor of yesterday's lunch. 'And the food was nice too.'

'I prefer to give my full attention to the woman I am with,' he replied, walking her across the pavement to where his car sat squatting on double yellow lines.

He opened the door, saw her inside and settled before walking around the long, low bonnet of the car to the driver's side. And through it all, Natalia was acutely aware that the ordinary conversation and the polite way they were treating each other were all just a front to cover up what was really happening here.

Giancarlo settled himself in the seat next to her, and she couldn't resist watching him as he did what was necessary to set them in motion. The suit was black, silk sheened and so obviously stylish that she didn't doubt for a second that it had begun life in the gifted hands of some famous Italian designer. In profile his face was even more attractive than it was full on—which surprised her when she thought about his less than perfect nose.

He turned his head, caught the intent way she was looking at him. 'What?' he asked curiously.

'Why didn't you come up?' The question came out as a low and husky quaver.

His eyes grew dark. 'You know why,' he replied. 'For the same reason I did not allow myself to do this, in the foyer.' Then he leaned across and kissed her.

It was the most beautiful moment she had ever experienced with him, nothing forced, no fighting—with herself or him—but a kiss conveying a promise she knew she would not attempt to resist when the moment finally came to her.

Their tongues touched, just once, then he was drawing away again, his eyes warm on hers as he brought up his hand and gently rubbed his thumb pad over her still parted, slightly pulsing lips, once, twice, three times, then he kissed her again.

'I prefer the taste of you to your lipstick,' he murmured when he drew away a second time.

After that she sat there while he drove, quietly coming to terms with the knowledge that something had just changed between them. She didn't know what it was, she only knew that she liked it.

He parked the car in a side street not far from his apartment, then took her in through a discreet door that led down into a basement club with low lighting and the kind of rhythmic blues music that kept pace with the throb of her pulse. They were shown to a table over in a corner with barely no more light than the candle in its centre where they ate seafood pasta from a plate they shared together, followed by chicken in a creamy sauce made in heaven.

And they talked, softly—carefully at first until they learned to relax with each other a little, their faces shrouded by a darkness lit only by the candlelight but no less alluring, because the mood was like that. Maybe the wine he insisted she have helped, even though he thoughtfully diluted it with sparkling water.

'I'm driving.' He smiled when she showed surprise to see him watering down his wine too...

But they both knew there was much more to it than that. He wanted her fully conscious and aware of everything they did tonight. He wanted no misunderstandings as to why she was going to allow him to make love to her. It was too essential to his plan that she came to him openly and willingly to place it in jeopardy by plying her with alcohol she had already admitted she didn't have a head for.

Then—hell, he thought. It was essential to *him* that she came to him clear-headed and knowingly!

'Let's dance,' he said on impulse, drawing her to her feet before she could argue.

He wanted to feel her close, run his hands over her body. He wanted to hold her into the cradle of his hips while they danced to something slow and easy, feel her moving against him, and just lose himself in the smoky promise in her eyes.

And he wanted to feel the sweet sting of desire build and build until neither of them could stand it any longer, then relieve the tension in hours of mind-blowing passion that would meld her to him so completely that she would never want him to let go of her again.

So he led her across the room to a tiny dance floor in front of the live blues band supplying the music, turned her into his arms and felt the instant tremor of electricity begin passing from her to him then back again.

It told him enough—for now. On a sigh that conveyed his pleasure in having her close, he used a hand on her waist to bring her against him, then began moving them to the swaying pulse of the music, with the feel of her breath on his throat, and his hands stroking the silk-covered framework of the most desirable woman he had ever held in his arms...

What made it all so much more sweetly tortuous was that she loved being this close to him. It was utterly intoxicating—more so than any mere glass of wine when the music seemed to throb to a beat she felt was being generated by the two of them rather than the live band on the podium.

She could feel the need in him talking to the need in her. It was all so compelling, even the way she let her fingers glide from his breastplate to his shoulders was an act compelled by a force she had no control over.

The action stretched her body, arched her back into closer contact with what was beginning to happen to him. Yet he didn't attempt to ease her away, and they swayed like that for what seemed like for ever, until she couldn't stand it any more and lifted her face up as he was lowering his to look at her.

What she saw written there held the air trapped in her lungs. It was desire, pure and simple, hot and tight.

'Let's get out of here,' he murmured, and even the rough-toned command had an arousing effect on her.

'Yes,' she answered. That was all, and she found herself being guided back to their table where he helped her into her jacket then walked her towards the exit, pausing only long enough to pay the bill.

Outside it was dry but cold and she stood shivering while he unlocked the car and helped her inside. He drove them away in silence, and headed for his apartment in silence. The fact that she wasn't voicing a protest told them both everything they needed to know.

The car swooped down into the basement then into its reserved bay. The engine died, he didn't look at her and she was glad because she didn't think she had the courage to look at him.

This kind of situation was so very new to her. She might not be a complete novice, but neither was she versed in the kind of artistry she suspected was required of sophisticated affairs.

And that was exactly what this was going to be, she told herself firmly—a sophisticated affair into which both partners entered knowing the eventual outcome.

A glorious time of loving, then the sad farewell.

She could do it; she knew the rules even if she had never played by them before! And those were the rules she *wanted* to play by. She had no choice. She could not allow herself to ever *hope* there was another choice.

He opened his door and climbed out. She did the same on the other side of the car. Then they walked together—yet oddly apart—into the waiting lift, and rode it all the way up to his apartment without either uttering a single word as to what was about to happen.

Strange, Natalia decided, understanding her own need to stay quiet in case she said something that would show him just how nervous she was feeling about this. But his silence worried her, for surely a man with his experience knew how important it was to keep the mood alive?

Yet he was standing there, frowning down at his feet as if something was bothering him but he didn't know how to voice his concerns.

Had he changed his mind? she wondered suddenly. Had the simple act of getting her to come here with him freely and willingly killed whatever it was that had been driving him to get her to this point?

The lift stopped; the doors slid open. Neither of them moved. Then he looked up—directly into her wary eyes. 'This is no game we are playing here, Natalia,' he said very seriously.

It made her frown because there hadn't been a single moment since she'd met him that she'd thought any of this a *game*.

'I am a very possessive man. If you stay with me now, you will belong to me. I will not tolerate anything less than your full commitment to me for as long as this thing lasts between us.'

He was talking more than a one-night stand here—

which was a relief because she hadn't been sure, not when their feelings had been running so hot and fevered from the beginning.

And 'as long as this thing lasts' suited her perfectly. Better than a one-night stand, but also better than a fear of something deeper developing. For that could never happen—could not be allowed to happen.

'I understand,' she said.

Relief tautened the flesh across his chest muscles. But it did nothing for the silent war he was having with himself. One part of him wanted to just tell her to go, get out of here while she still had the chance to leave relatively unscathed.

But another part of him was yelling at him not to be a bloody fool! Take what was on offer and let the future sort itself out!

He didn't understand himself, didn't understand what had suddenly altered inside him from the moment he'd begun the drive home. He wanted her, for goodness' sake! So, what was the problem?

Inviting her to leave the lift in front of him, he watched her body move with that sensual grace he had been watching for days now with a tightness around his loins.

Get yourself together, man! he told himself angrily. Then, 'Natalia,' he said.

She stopped, then turned. His heart skipped a beat, then began pounding in his chest. She looked frighteningly uncertain all of a sudden. He didn't blame her for feeling that way after the stupid performance he had just put on.

And why had he done that? He no longer knew because he was looking at that sensational figure draped in the same colour as her eyes, and the heat that went whistling through him put his mind right back in focus.

'The white,' he drawled lazily, relaxing his face muscles into a more seductive expression.

'White?' she repeated blankly. Then she caught on and blushed.

'The black was too provocative and the red was too—hot, so it has to be the white.'

Refusing to answer him, she turned away and stalked off towards the sitting room with her cheeks still on fire.

He was on fire again. He was even grinning as he paced after her. Without a word, he diverted into the kitchen, saw the champagne waiting in its bucket of melted ice, and the grin grew wider because he was perfectly happy again.

Edward didn't matter. Her *feelings* for Edward didn't matter—if that was what had been bothering him so much back there…

Natalia removed her jacket and draped it over one of the white leather chairs, then began pacing the sunken area with a tension that showed in her face.

She shouldn't be here with him. His strange attitude before had tugged a bit of sanity to the fore. It was wrong. It was dangerous. He belonged to the enemy camp. What happened if Edward ever found out? What would her being with Giancarlo Cardinale, of all men, do to him?

She should leave, she told herself. Now, while she had the chance to do it without having to explain herself. He'd disappeared, she didn't know where. She could just pick up her things and run.

Then what? asked the voice of reason. What happens tomorrow—do you hide away in your little house so he can't get you, and lose your job in the interim? How would you explain *that* away to Edward on his return without making Giancarlo look like the bad guy in all of this, when in actual fact it's you who is being bad here?

And—do you want him or don't you want him? she then asked herself impatiently. For those are the only two questions which should really count. After all, you can't go on for ever running your life to suit Edward's feelings. Especially when Edward was not willing to run his life according to yours!

So—do you want Giancarlo Cardinale, or don't you want him?

He appeared in the opening. He had done it again, was the first disturbing thing she thought. His jacket had gone, so had his tie, and the top two buttons on his shirt had been tugged undone. The wretched man had a habit of half undressing in her company that always managed to shatter her composure.

Or what bit of composure she ever possessed around him, she wryly expanded, noticing that he was also carrying the bottle of champagne and two fluted glasses which acted as yet another trigger, flipping her mind like a coin from one face to another.

Yes, I want this man, the new face said. Yes, I *need* this man! I can do this. I can love him and leave him when the time comes! I can—I *can*!

CHAPTER SEVEN

'HOLD that thought, whatever it is,' Giancarlo murmured lazily as he came down the steps to join Natalia.

He was smiling and relaxed, but the closer he came, the more tense she became, because, now it came right down to it, she didn't think she could carry this through with the *savoir-faire* he was probably expecting.

Maybe he sensed it, because there was a curious expression in his eyes as he came to stand beside her, and, although his attention was mainly involved in putting the two glasses down on the marble table so he could begin pouring champagne, he kept on sending her the odd glance, as if he couldn't quite make his mind up what it was that made her tick inside.

She wished she knew herself but sadly she didn't, or she would know how she should be behaving. Was she supposed to indulge in some light conversation to bridge the gap between this moment and the one where they moved on to the bedroom? Or should she be making certain moves on him to encourage along that second stage?

It didn't really matter because neither suggestion was possible for her right now. She felt too out of her depth, too tongue-tied by too little experience and especially with a man like him.

Picking up the two frothing glasses, he turned to hand one of them to her. She took it, eyes lowered now because that seemed the easiest way to get through these next few telling minutes.

'Sip,' he commanded.

Obediently, she sipped while he watched with a new kind of stillness that brought the colour streaking into her cheeks. The champagne tingled on her tongue, then did the same all the way to her stomach.

'Again,' he said and received mute obedience a second time.

He waited until she had made her second swallow, then his hand came to gently lift her chin—and he was no longer smiling. 'Last chance, *cara*,' he murmured quietly. 'I must be sure that this is what you want.'

Was it? she asked herself. Was jumping in the deep end when she barely knew how to swim what she really wanted to do? No, not really. 'Yes,' she whispered. 'This is what I want.'

'Then why the sudden look of anxiety?' he prompted.

'You told me to hold the thought,' she wryly pointed out.

'That belonged to a different thought,' he returned. 'I am now discussing the one that denies me your eyes.'

Lifting her lashes, she looked directly into his dark and sombre eyes and smiled a wry smile at his even needing to ask that question. 'I've known you for less than a week, and you wonder why I am anxious about this?'

'Would a few more days make any difference?' He put the question to her with genuine interest, she was sure, but it was mocking all the same, because he knew just as she knew that *this* had been written on the wall from the first second of their first glance at each other.

'No,' she ruefully replied.

'Then keep those beautiful eyes on me,' he softly commanded. 'I like to make love with *all* the senses, and your eyes make love to me more than any other pair of eyes I've known.'

'Known many?' she asked in a lightly mocking attempt to sound clever and witty and sophisticated.

His smile reappeared, teasing and warm. 'No, this is my first time,' he said.

And she laughed. It was such an outrageous thing to say—and she felt some of her awkwardness seep away. I love you, she wanted to say, but those words were banned to her every which way she looked at them, so she did the next best thing and reached up on tiptoe to brush her mouth against his.

'A lady has a right to be unsure of herself at moments like this,' she murmured as she drew away again.

'So does a man,' he countered. 'Now—take a sip of your champagne again and hold it in your mouth.'

Intrigued by the instruction, she did as he bade, her eyes still fixed on his as he did the same thing with his champagne. Champagne bubbles began to fizz on her tongue and the roof of her mouth, and the air between them stirred as a new level of awareness took precedence.

Lost in the warmth of his eyes and the awakening of her own desires, she therefore didn't see what was coming until it was too late. With a smooth, slick move he slid a hand around her waist—then swooped on her mouth with no warning whatsoever.

The result was an explosion on the senses when his champagne-moistened tongue made contact with hers. It was the most erotic thing she had ever experienced. In a single moment she seemed to shoot from gentle awareness into full arousal with no gap in between. Her hand shot up, instinctively searching for support as pure sensation went racing through her on the flow of champagne bubbles that had entered her blood.

Her hand found a tightly muscled shoulder, and gripped. Breathing had gone haywire, mouth hot on mouth. Nervous barriers fell, uncertainties disappeared. The kiss deepened and became something else entirely—seduction at its most intense.

She heard the light tap of glass on stone but didn't recognise the sound for what it was until she felt her own glass being taken from her and placed on the marble table. Freedom to use both hands had her moving closer to him with her fingers sliding up the front of his shirt. She felt the warmth of living flesh, the hardness of well-honed muscle, and the slight prickle of chest hair, all of which sent a pleasurable little sigh whispering from her mouth into his mouth.

Why the champagne kiss should have caused this to happen, she didn't understand. All she knew was that it had happened—and that he'd known it was going to happen, which automatically said he had done this before.

'You're too good at this,' she murmured unsteadily when he eventually let their mouths separate.

'I get even better,' was his conceited reply. Then, with only that mocking remark to accompany them, he caught her hand and began leading her up the steps towards the waiting bedroom. As they passed by the wall switch he paused to dim the sitting-room lights. In the bedroom he did the same, shrouding them in a more intimate atmosphere, then taking her back into his arms.

She went without a murmur, her mouth welcoming him as if they were already lovers. The bed was several yards away, but neither seemed in any rush to get there, so it was reached in easy stages, the first stage being the caressing way he began to remove her dress. His hands skimmed her body, lighting fires as they went, then fed the flames on their way back up again. Long fingers slid beneath the silken weight of her hair swinging gently away from her back because of the passionate tilt of her head.

He found her nape, used his fingers to lightly measure its slenderness, then was moving again, finding the zip to her dress and drawing it downwards, while she merely clung to him, needing his strength when her limbs began to shimmer with a sultry kind of heat.

Then he was diverting her attention again by peeling her dress down her arms and her body until she stood in front of him in nothing but what she was wearing beneath. So now he knew his provocative guess earlier had been absolutely right, she realised as she watched his dark gaze skim over her white silk underwear with a look of triumph he did nothing to disguise.

'Homework?' he taunted softly, and she began blushing like crazy.

He just laughed huskily, and proceeded to make her feel utterly wanton standing there with her dress pooled around her feet as he explored every silk-smooth inch of her while retaining both his clothes and his dignity.

Not for long though, not for long. For it didn't take many seconds for her fingers to release the rest of the buttons on his shirt. He lost her mouth as the two pieces of fine white linen parted and a need to look at him overrode her need to feel his mouth seducing hers...

The last thing he expected her to do was to stroke him as he had been stroking her. The feel of her fingers against his flesh had his chest expanding on a fierce intake of air. The fingers paused, her eyes flickered upward to catch the intense pleasure reflected in his, then, with a sensuality that knocked him sideways, she moistened her softly pulsing mouth with the tip of her tongue, then lowered her gaze again and leaned forward to begin stringing clinging kisses from one tight male nipple to the other.

'*Dio, cara,*' he breathed in shaken reaction. And closed

his eyes as her mouth, her tongue and her caressing fingers locked him into his own world of burgeoning pleasure...

She'd been wanting to touch him like this for so long now it felt like for ever, Natalia was thinking hazily. And he was so wonderful to touch. She could feel his response in each ripple of flesh she so carefully explored. His breathing was tight, his heart thumping against his solid ribcage, and her fingertips felt enlivened by the rasping sensation of crisp body hair and satin tight flesh.

She wanted more. And more came with her lips joining in the banquet. At the first moist touch of her tongue on his skin he opened his eyes again, looked deeply into hers, then muttered something in his own language as she shook his hands free of the shirt so he could reach for her...

Mouths joined again, hotly, hungrily, her arms looped around his neck. Finding her slender hips, he eased her up against him, then leaned back against the wall behind to simply sink himself into the rousing heat permeating his body as she began to move against him in an erotic rhythm no man with blood in his veins could resist.

She was a born sensualist, and he couldn't believe his luck in finding someone like her. Inhibition seemed like a foreign word to her. She wanted him and was doing absolutely nothing to disguise that want. Did Edward know her like this?

No! his mind blasted angrily back at him. You fool, don't bring him in here!

'What—what's wrong?' Feeling the violent change in him sent her jerking back from him in confused reaction.

'Niente,' he rasped, didn't even know he had spoken in Italian, but saw her beautiful eyes darken into wariness and, on a grim act of black fury aimed entirely at himself

for ruining the moment, he bent to scoop her up into his arms. 'I want you, that is what is wrong,' he growled. 'Have you any idea what you are doing to me?'

'Yes,' she said, and it shut down his anger like a plug being pulled on something destructive.

Because there it was—the look in her eyes he had first seen long days ago and had been searching for ever since. It was warm, it was soft, it was steamy and sultry and reminded him of the goal he had set himself to learn what happened to her eyes when he was deep inside her and she was toppling over the edge...

'Yes...' he agreed on a sensual hiss that made her tremble because she knew he was turning the answer right back on herself.

For he knew what he was doing to her, and as she gazed up into his velvet dark eyes, with their fires of desire burning inside, she knew she was about to be drawn into the flame.

He was taking over. He had been playing it passively for a while but now he became the man she'd expected, dark and demanding, holding her eyes by sheer strength of will as he reached for the hand she still had linked around his neck, and, being very deliberate about it, he drew the hand down between their two bodies and placed it on the clasp to his trousers.

It was a command to finish undressing him, and heat prickled along her skin. If he saw her uncertainty he wasn't letting her keep it. 'Do it,' he urged her and lifted his own hands to her shoulders, where long fingers hooked beneath narrow bra straps and with an agonising slowness he began drawing them down the curve of her arms.

It was a mutual undressing which heightened the tension to its nth degree. Tiny lace cups folded away from two high, firm, perfect breasts that clearly didn't need the support anyway. She released a sharp gasp when he first touched her there, running feather-like caresses over newly exposed flesh that responded by swelling and tightening with pleasure...

'Do it,' he repeated, keeping her mind focused on her own task, even if she didn't want it to be. 'Undress me,' he urged. 'Touch me. I want to feel what you feel...'

He could see what she was feeling because her head had tipped back and her mouth had parted and she was barely functioning on a conscious level. So when her fingers began to move against his waist, it felt like a small victory to be able to command her even while she was lost like this.

But it was a brief victory, he realised, feeling the muscles around his waist contract forcefully when her nails inadvertently rasped against his flesh. Sensation went raking through him, hot enough and tight enough to clench muscles all over him. *Dio*, he thought, and she hasn't even touched me where it matters yet...

It was all so erotic. While her fingers fumbled with the catch on his trousers, he was running tormenting forays across her acutely taut nipples with his fingertips. And her breathing was hectic; she couldn't think beyond the crazy notion that if this was making love the Sicilian way, then how did any woman survive it?

You don't know if you will yet, a little voice inside her head dryly taunted. This is only the beginning; wait until he decides to move to the really heavy stuff.

Stuff like lowering his dark head to kiss her hotly as she began to draw his zip down and felt the backs of her fingers make contact with a hard male erection covered by only the thin fabric of his undershorts. The experience made the centre of her sex begin to pulse to a beat of its own making, or maybe it was his beat, she was no longer sure of anything worth a damn. The whole affair was beginning to grow very steamy, his mouth hot and demanding on her mouth, his fingers tormenting her breasts and his manhood playing havoc with any preconceptions she might have had about his prowess in that area of his physical make-up.

She failed the major test though, because for the life of her she couldn't get herself to peel down those shorts. Or maybe he was the one that relented, she thought dazedly when, on a sudden decision that seemed to come from nowhere, he unclipped her bra, discarded it to the floor, then lifted her into his arms and carried her to the bed. Carefully lowering her onto it, he stood back to begin removing the rest of his clothes himself while she curled onto her side and lay there watching the deliberate strip-show taking place.

His shoes left his feet, the trousers were stripped away along with undershorts and socks in a few swift economical moves that quite simply took her breath away. But not as the sight of his body did, its leanness and its strength and the arrogance with which he displayed it all culminating in turning the excitement she was experiencing up another notch…

He saw it happen, saw the flame light her eyes and felt suddenly charged with sheer masculine pride in what she was seeing. But then, the feeling was mutual. She was lying here on his bed at last, and as he came down beside her his heart was thundering because she was the one who was reaching for him.

Everything merged into one long glorious coming-together after that. Her hands moved on his body, and his lips sought her breasts and the delicate round of her navel so exquisitely sensitive to the lap of his tongue. And she was anxiously kneading his shoulders when he began to slide the last flimsy scrap of silk down her hips.

'Kiss me,' she groaned.

It was such a desperate little command that he stretched up to take her mouth with a hungry passion that she simply sank herself into while he continued caressing each new section of flesh he was exposing. When his finger finally made contact with the soft mound of curls at the apex of her sex, he felt the fine, tight shudder of pleasure ripple through her, and was overawed by how good it made him feel.

And it wasn't all one-sided because her hands were moving over his body, tracing restlessly the length of his back, the lean tightness of his buttocks, his hair-roughened thighs, and he found himself willing her to put him out of his agony and take him in hand. It became a kind of battle, while their mouths clung and their bodies writhed, and their fingers hovered just beyond the goal both of them desperately craved.

Who surrendered the battle first it was difficult to say; maybe it was a joint surrender, because as he felt the tip of his finger slide that extra inch into sheer, sweet luxury her fingers closed around him with a delicate tenderness that rocked him to the core.

Her few scraps of clothing were an irritant now. With a rough sound of impatience he pushed himself up and completely rid her of her white panties. The stockings came next, sliding off silken legs which aided him by lifting and flexing in a way that almost sent him over the edge. He caught one long, slender calf in his hand and bowed his mouth to it, hungrily, sucking and biting his way upwards—until she stopped him by the simple act of pulling him by his hair back down beside her.

And in that one urgent movement, everything changed yet again. They looked deep into each other's eyes and it acted like a gentle calming, everything slowed to a long, lazy touch, feel, teasing medley. She kissed his eyelids, his cheeks, his arrogant nose, and smiled softly when he returned the honour.

'Beautiful,' he whispered, stroking his fingers through the silken spread of her hair. 'You take my breath away.'

'So do you,' she softly confided.

He laughed, softly. Then suddenly he wasn't laughing, he was kissing her hot and deep, and the whole thing became charged again, but with serious intent this time. Caresses became bold, more intimate, until they were touching each other with an urgency that could only be assuaged one way.

He came over her, she welcomed him, he settled his lean hips between her clinging thighs, and as he prepared to join them she seemed to know that he wanted her to open her eyes, and to keep on looking at him as that joining became real with the single deep thrust of his hips.

His eyes were black, glittering down at her, his features taut with desire. He began to move, slowly, deeply, watched the telling darkening of her own eyes as he built the pulsing pleasure at his own rich pace. Her legs had locked themselves around his body, her slender arms clinging to his back. And as the urgency grew in both of them still their eyes did not break contact; it was part of the loving, a necessary part, another point of total communication where they spoke to each other with every sense but without words.

Her eyes held no blue any more, only smoky swirls of grey and black, and even the grey was losing ground the closer she came to that final leap. And her mouth was open, the tense little gasps of pleasure growing thicker, more arousing when he'd thought he could never be more aroused.

But Natalia Deyton could make him feel things he had never felt before. She was warm and she was generous, and she held nothing in reserve. When his breathing grew tense and the rhythm became stronger, she simply came with him—all the way—stroke for stroke, shudder for exquisite shudder. Her hands shot up, grasped his face, her eyes spiralling out that final hint of grey as her body quickened. Then, 'Giancarlo,' she breathed.

That was all. Just his name in that soul-stripping way, then she leapt—*Dio,* she leapt, on a convulsion of muscle that completely shattered him—and shot him into the same wild place still echoing with his name as if she was pulling him with her into the kind of climax that took him way beyond anything he had ever experienced.

The woman was a witch. *His* witch, was the final fiercely possessive thought he had before he lost himself in the hot, dark bounty of their shared release...

Lying there beneath him with his face now pressed into the side of her throat and her body still pulsing gently around his possession, Natalia closed her eyes and just let herself float on a lazy sea of satiation. His weight was heavy on her but she didn't mind—she felt wonderfully invaded by his heat and his scent and an awareness that both of them were lying stretched out without a single bone between them that hadn't gone weak.

A smile touched her mouth, though she tried to stop it.

'Shh,' he breathed against her throat as if he was afraid she was about to speak and spoil the moment.

But that was her very last intention; she felt too good,

too at peace, too at one with this lover of hers who had given as much as he had taken. It was a beautiful knowledge. And just as beautiful to know from that lazy 'shh' that he was feeling the same way about it.

Eventually they moved, though, eventually with seemingly perfect sensory co-ordination he withdrew from her just as she reached the point where she needed to stretch her limbs to encourage them to recover some substance. With a lazy kiss pressed to her throat, he slid himself sideways, bent a knee across her thighs as if to make sure she didn't decide to stray, then came up on one elbow to look down on her gravely while gentle fingers carefully combed stray locks of her hair away from her face and throat and shoulders.

It was an act of tenderness she had not expected, and her throat tightened slightly on a tug of emotion as she lay there.

'You said my name,' he murmured suddenly.

Her long lashes flickered on a blink of surprise. 'I did?' she responded, having no memory of saying anything, she had been so lost to her senses.

He smiled an oddly satisfied smile. '*Sí*,' he confirmed. 'You called for me, Giancarlo, at your moment of ecstasy. It—pleased me.'

She could see that it did. But the remark still confused her. 'Who else did you expect me to call for?' she enquired with a little frown and teasing glint of amusement.

His response threw her. Instead of coming up with some answering tease to keep the same soft, intimate mood flowing, his face hardened and he growled something harsh in his own language, then swooped on her mouth with the kind of kiss that staked a claim she didn't think was necessary since he already possessed her.

'Mine,' he reiterated fiercely when he drew away again.

'You are *my* woman now, you understand me? You think only of me, you say only my name, and you dream only of me, *comprende*?'

'Oh, very possessive,' she mocked, not sure whether to be pleased by the burst of jealous possessiveness or angry at him for feeling he needed to stake his claim!

'*Sí,*' he confirmed, no shame, no apology. 'I am Sicilian,' he added with a lift of his chin that seemed to be conveying something portentous in that announcement. 'I guard what belongs to me.'

'And you think I now belong to you, is that it?'

'*Sí.*'

'And who do you belong to?'

'You, of course.' He frowned as if he didn't see the necessity for the question.

Which was Natalia's point, because neither did she see the necessity for this conversation at all! Unless this was his roundabout way of getting down to laying out the ground rules, she then thought on a sudden tight sting of understanding. 'How long for?' she asked huskily.

His frown darkened. 'For as long as it lasts, I suppose,' he answered. 'Who can say?' he added with what she supposed was a very Sicilian noncommittal shrug to go with his question.

But the shrug came too late, because Natalia was already ahead of him, ahead and walking along the self-same line. 'S-six weeks,' she heard herself say in a breathless tense little whisper, needing now to lay out the terms of this affair before he did it for her. 'When Edward comes back, you go home, and this will be over...'

Edward—? She dared to bring Edward, here, into *his* bed after what they had just shared? She dared to speak

Edward's name? Lay her rules about the length of their affair before him—in words that revolved around Edward?

Like a man who had just been attacked by a snake, he flinched right back from her, his eyes turning black as the vision in front of him changed from beauty personified in his eyes into Medusa—turning him into a pillar of stone where he lay.

Nothing that had ever happened to him before had made him feel as bad as he did right now. For here they were, having only just recovered from one of the most passionate interludes life could offer—and she was bartering terms like a whore in the market place. But with those terms revolving around *Edward*?

Anger suddenly roared, pumping the life right back into his frozen limbs to help throw his body round until he was looming threateningly over her. Unsure at this point if he was going to strangle her or kiss her darling Edward right out of existence, he reached for her shoulders.

She stiffened in alarm. 'What did I do? What did I say?' she begged in complete bewilderment as to why he was suddenly so angry. In her view, he supposed, she had just handed him the perfect excuse for dumping her and he should be damn well singing in elation!

But he wasn't singing, he was seething, because she had just confirmed every low, cheap, nasty thing he had ever been told about her. Brazen wasn't in it. 'You dare to set boundaries of time around me,' he bit out thickly, 'as if I am a stud bull in a field lingering with the female currently in line to be serviced—and then wonder why I am angry?'

She went quite white, and so she should do, he acknowledged as he watched remorse darken her beautiful eyes. 'I'm sorry,' she breathed. 'I didn't mean... I just thought you—'

'Well, don't think,' he growled. 'Not in my bed—ever!'

Then, because he couldn't stop himself, he buried his mouth in hers and wished to God he knew where this was going to take him, because something nasty was warning him that he was in too deep.

Natalia Deyton was beginning to get to him in ways he just hadn't expected...

CHAPTER EIGHT

NATALIA had offended Giancarlo and she hadn't meant to do that. In fact the last thing she ever wanted to do was spoil what had been the most beautiful experience of her life.

So when he kissed her she kissed him back hungrily. He was angry, so the kiss was rough, but the anger also ignited other emotions, which soon began to take them over.

For a second experience so soon after the first, it really should have been disappointing. But it seemed as if nothing this man could do would ever disappoint her. He drove deep and she welcomed his potency. He kissed hard and long and she fed it all back to him. They touched and tasted and lost touch with everything but themselves to an extent that it didn't even register that they were doing all of this without a single thought to protection.

That singularly terrifying occurrence happened when she was standing in his bathroom, carefully drying tender places after their shower in which their third wild coming together had taken them tumbling over the edge of sanity.

'Oh, no,' she whispered, going so still that it was no wonder he spun sharply to face her.

He was standing by the bathroom mirror with a towel looped casually around his lean waist while he used an electric razor, but the sound stopped abruptly when he saw her expression. 'What?' he demanded. 'What have you done?' His eyes dipped down to where her hand was tensely crushing the towel, then blackened in concern as they flicked back to her face again. 'Did I hurt you, *cara*?' he questioned jerkily.

She shook her head, her face so white it could have been porcelain. 'Y-you didn't use anything,' she managed to utter.

He froze, frowning, then slowly put down the razor to begin walking towards her. 'This is a joke, right,' he murmured.

But he had to know that it wasn't. She still hadn't moved and didn't think she dared to. Her legs felt strange, as if they were just about ready to give out on her, and her heart was labouring to find a steady rhythm.

'No,' she breathed, and began to shiver as shock thoroughly took her over.

Several Italian curses hit her eardrums, but he made a grab for a fresh towel and quickly wrapped it around her before grimly picking her up and carrying her back into the bedroom.

He sat her down on the bed, then swung round to sit down heavily beside her. He was in shock too, she recognised. Or maybe she should describe it as horror. 'How could we have been so blind stupid?' she choked.

'You are on the pill,' he bit out tautly. '*All* women take the pill!'

'Well, not this one!' she shot back, fiercely and furiously. 'God—' she jumped up. 'I should have known this was going to turn nasty on me! You're the wrong man for me! We shouldn't even have been doing this—!'

'I am *not* the wrong man for you!' he barked, instantly offended by the suggestion.

But he didn't understand and she couldn't explain it to him, so she began pacing the floor with the towel huddled round her, trying to come to terms with the dreadful fact that she might well already be pregnant with Edward's wife's brother's child!

'Oh.' The whimper was one of dismay and helplessness. 'Why didn't you think to ask?' she suddenly launched at him.

He was white behind the olive tint of his skin and his eyes were angry. 'Why did you not think to say?' he tossed back with biting derision.

'Because I did believe that most intelligent men thought safe sex a natural precaution!' she spat back, not knowing why she was attacking him like this when she knew she was as much to blame.

He jerked to his feet, and she instantly felt wretched because his cheekbones were no longer pale but dark with embarrassment. There seemed nothing left to say. As he walked off towards the bathroom again, she began gathering her scattered clothes together in a dazed kind of way that said she didn't know what she was doing.

By the time he came back a few minutes later he seemed to have himself back in control while she was just standing there staring blindly down at the few scraps of white silk she held in her hands, as if she didn't know how they'd got there.

'I'm sorry,' she whispered when she felt him in front of her. 'This is my fault. I should have thought...'

'Ditto,' Giancarlo replied and wondered why he wasn't feeling anything more than a rueful acceptance for his tragic lot.

Because she looked so adoringly pathetic? Because she was right and he should have been more careful—for his own health's sake if nothing else?

Or was it because her shrill claim that he was the wrong man for her had struck at the very heart of his ego and made it more important to him to prove her wrong about that than to stand about in a horrified stupor, wondering how the hell he was going to extricate himself from this potential disaster?

'What is the timing like?' he asked, gently extracting the bits of silk from her fingers while she let him because his question had made her pause and take stock of the situation.

'Good,' she murmured eventually. 'Good as in low risk,' she then extended, which made him grimace because *good* could only mean that—in this case anyway.

'Right,' he acknowledged. 'Then we have a wait-and-see situation on our hands,' and he smoothly whipped the towel away from her shoulders.

'What are you doing?' she cried, making an attempt to grab it back again.

Too late, for he was already tossing it to one side along with her clothes. 'Taking you back to bed,' he said so casually that it even surprised him how calmly he was behaving. He grasped one of her hands. 'It is three o'clock in the morning and we both need some sleep.'

'Sleep?' she repeated.

He turned a grin on her that had her eyes widening. 'Sleep,' he repeated. 'You've ravished me enough for one night.'

'But—' she was floundering and he liked it '—I should be going home and—'

It was the simplest thing in the world to swing her down on the bed then follow her. 'Home is here now,' he smoothly decreed. 'For the next few weeks anyway until we know one way or another.'

'What are you talking about?' she protested. 'I don't need to live here with you just because we have both behaved recklessly!'

'Yes, you do,' he insisted, stripping the towel from his hips and tossing it aside before he reached for the sheet to cover them. 'I am Sicilian. I take care of my own. And until you prove otherwise, you now belong to me—so don't even think about taking a morning-after pill. And also,' he added with husky promise, 'I want you here. Can you tell me honestly that you do not want to be here too?'

She couldn't. He knew it. She might claim he was the wrong man for her, but when it came down to it he was the one she wanted.

The only thing she said was, 'I had no intention of taking a morning-after pill. I don't agree with them.'

Reaching across her to put out the light, he kissed her delicious mouth as he settled down beside her, then pulled her into his arms.

'Tomorrow we move your things in,' he said softly into the darkness.

She didn't say another word.

He had her. She didn't know it yet, but he had Natalia Deyton just where he wanted her and, despite the stupid risks it had taken to get her here, he had never felt so good about anything...

To her own surprise, Natalia slept heavily, waking up to find herself alone in the bed as a weak sun began seeping in through the voile-draped windows. She lay there for a while, listening to the warm quietness surrounding her, reluctant to let herself begin thinking of the calamitous events of the night before.

Though not all of them had been calamitous, she admitted, feeling an accompanying warmth filter into those places in her body that had known only pleasure last night. In fact some of those moments had been so intense that it was impossible not to soften and allow them to replay themselves for a little while.

But only a little while, she accepted when a sound from somewhere beyond the bedroom alerted her to the fact that she was not alone here. Giancarlo must be around somewhere, waiting for her to put in an appearance.

A sigh whispered from her, dragging her out of her relaxed stupor and forcing her to get out of bed where she padded off to use the bathroom before going in search of her suit bag, so she could put back on the clothes she had arrived here in yesterday.

They seemed more appropriate somehow, now that daylight was back and with it reality. The slinky blue dress and the sexy underwear belonged to another time and most definitely another person than the one she was seeing in the mirror this morning.

And just who was she seeing? she asked herself as she stood, carefully pleating her hair with the knowledge that she was using the severe style as a piece of armour.

A very foolish woman, she informed herself, who had made a huge mistake that was now clawing at her conscience and grating at worries she should never have put aside in the first place.

Namely—Edward versus Giancarlo Cardinale. Even the name made her feel chill now.

Not the man, though, she admitted as she watched her eyes darken simply by conjuring up his image. The man in his full and physical sense had never been the problem for her. It was his name and his relationship to Edward that caused this impossible conflict she could see no way round whichever way she tried to look at it.

Not that it really mattered now, she supposed, turning to pull on her clothes and make herself presentable. The whole thing had turned sour from the moment she'd realised that neither had thought about contraception.

Oh, he had been good and kind and said all the right things a woman he had just made love to would expect from a real man. But there was no way in the cold light of day that she was going to hold him to any of them. She could only hope that in the cold light of the same day he, too, had thought better about bringing his new lover here to live with him when surely the quick exit and a lot of inner praying was the best way to be dealing with this?

With those very wise thoughts in mind, she slipped her feet into low black court shoes and made herself go in search of him. She found him lounging at the kitchen table with the *Financial Times* spread open in front of him and a pot of coffee at his elbow.

He looked different this morning, she noted as she paused in the doorway. His clothes were different. Casual chinos and a long-sleeved polo shirt in a dark red colour that for some crazy reason reminded her of the red underwear he had provided yesterday and almost had her blushing.

Luckily the blush didn't arrive when, sensing her standing there, he looked up, and it only took him a few moments to run his eyes over her prim hairstyle and her equally prim slate-grey suit to know exactly what mood she was in this morning.

'Standing in guarded territory, I see,' he drawled, sitting back in his chair to view her more thoroughly. 'Tell me,' he appealed, 'that this does not declare an end to a beautiful friendship.'

'Don't be so trite,' she snapped, walking forwards and going to the fridge to get herself a carton of juice she had stashed in there yesterday, then opening cupboards until she found the glasses.

'Then don't try pulling any neat tricks on me, *cara*,' he replied with a sudden grimness. 'You belong to me now. We reached that agreement at some point in the early hours of this morning when we both knew what fools we had been.'

So, he was angry. She'd suspected as much by now—though she had expected the opposite response to it. 'Do you have any appointments today, or are you working from here?'

As a change of subject, she was rather pleased with the smooth way she did it—considering the butterflies going mad in her stomach. She even managed to pour the juice into the glass without spilling any of it onto the worktop.

'We are taking a day off,' he announced. 'So we can move your things in here.'

She put the juice carton down, and picked up the glass, aware that his angry eyes were still following every single thing she did as if he expected her to make a sudden run for it, and was not going to be caught napping when she did. 'I am not moving in here with you,' she told him quietly.

'After that we will do something really domestic, like supermarket shopping for provisions,' he went on as if she hadn't spoken.

'You can do that just as easily over the Internet these days,' she told him.

'Then there are a few things this place needs to make it more—homely,' he persisted unrelentingly. 'Like a television set and a decent music centre, and some cushions or something to make that soulless sitting room more inviting to relax in. And if you tell me that those can be ordered over the Internet,' he added with a silken snap, 'then I will probably have to stand up and come over there, and show you a few things that most certainly cannot!'

'Why are you so angry, for goodness' sake?' she turned to throw at him bewilderedly. 'You should be pleased I'm not keeping you to what you said last night…'

Giancarlo just glowered at her and said nothing, because how could he tell her that dear Edward had already been on his mobile asking where the hell his Natalia was? He was supposed to be patching up his marriage—the love-struck adulterer! Not worrying about his mistress because she wasn't exactly where he expected her to be!

So he'd lied to Edward and enjoyed doing it. He told him he'd sent her off on a fact-finding mission to some bloody place he couldn't even recall now. But it had served a dual purpose of reassuring Edward that not only was *his* Natalia safe, but she was also *safely* out of Giancarlo's influence!

The two-timing swine had actually said as much. And it stuck in his own throat that he couldn't just say— 'Go to hell, Edward. She is with me and staying with me! So keep your lecherous emotions in check from now on!'

But he couldn't say it, because he knew Edward. Let Edward know that he was aware of his little bit on the side and the stupid man would have a fit of panic and feel the need to confess all to Alegra just in case Giancarlo decided to do it before him! Edward knew how close brother and sister were and that any Sicilian male worth his salt would not remain silent in the face of such dishonour to one of his family!

But Giancarlo also knew that Alegra could not cope with the truth about her beloved Edward. She adored him—had adored him from the day he'd walked into her life at the tender age of eighteen, and no other man had ever come close to reaching her since! Unless you included Marco, he added with an ache that set his anger blazing.

For it was bad enough that she'd had to lose her son. To place in front of her the truth that she could be in danger of losing her husband would finish her. No doubt about it.

And to really top it all off nicely, he raged on within his own throbbing silence, he now knew, without a single doubt in his head, that if Edward had kept his lecherous hands to himself then he, Giancarlo, could have met Natalia Deyton and been free to explore the possibilities of their attraction with openness and honesty instead of having deceit and lies poisoning everything!

And the bottom line to that? he asked himself as his brain threatened to stall completely in response to his heated fury. He would not have rushed her into bed. And he would not have done it without even the most basic of sexual precautions!

So now he had a woman standing here who belonged to him in more ways than any woman had ever belonged to him, while she—

Hell! He stood up violently. She believed half of her still belonged to Edward! She even lived in Edward's house, damn it! Wore clothes bought with Edward's money!

Well, not for much longer, he vowed, his eyes hardening with a determination he could see was alarming her. But he had her. He had Natalia Deyton just where he wanted her. All he needed to do now was convince her of that!

'You could be carrying my child,' he reminded her thinly.

'There is just as much of a chance that I'm not!' she instantly replied.

'One chance in a thousand is good enough for me,' he returned. 'I am Sicilian,' he reiterated, knowing he was using his nationality like a damned hammer to beat her into submission. 'To a Sicilian, family is everything. While the small chance exists that you could be carrying my child, it makes you the mother of *my* Sicilian child! So stop arguing,' he said with the flick of a hand gauged to draw her anger. 'Accept your fate—for the near future anyway.'

'Why, you arrogant *bully*!' She gasped in wide-eyed disbelief that she was actually hearing any of this.

She was right and he was.

'I don't need to stand here and take this!'

Try moving, his eyes challenged. 'Drink your juice,' he prodded, saw the anger flare, saw the eyes change to warning bright diamonds, and was bracing himself for action even before the glass went sailing past his shoulder...

She couldn't believe she had just done that! Natalia stood staring in horrified amazement as the glass of juice went flying past his shoulder and smashed against the opposite set of wall units.

Trying to blink away the sense of shock, she ended up focusing on Giancarlo—then immediately wished she hadn't when she saw the expression his face was now wearing.

Retaliation was coming, she saw with a telling little quiver that had nothing to do with alarm. 'You asked for that,' she murmured unsteadily, feeding water onto burning oil when all he did was start striding towards her. 'Have you any idea how arrogant you sound? How self—' he reached her; in height and breadth and dangerous attitude he really intimidated enough to make her swallow nervously before she could carry on '—s-self-opinionated and just downright pompous?'

'Pompous,' he repeated, softly, smoothly, so succinctly she felt her fingernails digging into the underside of the unit top.

She nodded, swallowed again when his hand came up to rest on her shoulder, and stubbornly pretended that it wasn't there. 'Nobody th-these days goes around s-spouting such old-fashioned r-rubbish!'

'Rubbish,' he repeated that word also. And the hand moved from her shoulder to her nape. Natalia straightened her spine ever so warily. 'You think it is both rubbish and pompous to show a respect for family values?'

Values like his, she did, when she knew for an absolute fact that if he ever discovered her little secret he would soon forget those same family values. For there was no way that he would want to make *her* a part of his *Sicilian family* with or without his child inside her!

A point that didn't do her any favours at all because just thinking about it brought the sting of tears to the back of her eyes. 'You might pay my wages, Giancarlo—that does not give you the right to run my life!'

'No?' he said, and the hand at her nape tightened perceptibly, sending warning signals tingling down her spine. 'What about sex, then? Will the great sex be a big enough incentive to make you live with me?'

Live? That's a joke! she scoffed silently. He just wanted a convenient live-*in* sexual convenience! 'What, more studding for the prize bull?' she taunted. 'I thought that scenario offended your ego.'

'Well, let's just see, shall we?' he drawled lazily. And using his hand as a brace to lift her mouth up to his, his own swooped down and took...

Took without mercy, took by storm—took her shooting off to a place she didn't want to go to then never wanted to come back from.

Took her right there in the ultra-modern kitchen, with

her clothes gaping and her skirt ruched up around her waist
and the rest removed by very quick fingers.

And he took her with his mouth, nothing else. He took
her lips and her tongue and made him their master. He
took her breasts and teased and sucked until she cried out
in exquisite agony, and he took her down a dark, sensuous
road she had never ever dared to visit before when he bent
to her thighs and took the ultimate intimacy of all.

Which was when he took her will to fight him, right
there in the kitchen with her fingers laced into his hair and
her mind lost in a swirling sea of sensation.

'Giancarlo,' she begged. 'I'll do anything you say, but,
no more—please. I'll stay—I'll stay, but please make love
to me properly...'

And that was the point where she took something from
him. It was in his eyes when he rose, then picked her up
to carry her to the bedroom. She saw pain and remorse for
the tactic he'd used to gain her surrender. Then she saw
him begin a terrible battle with himself that she feared he
was actually going to win.

But he didn't. And, strangely, their lovemaking then was
the sweetest, gentlest, most deeply felt experience they had
shared to date.

Later, he dropped her off at her house with the promise
to be back in an hour to collect her. 'You won't come in
and wait?' she asked.

He looked at the house, then shook his dark head. 'No,
I won't come in,' he answered. 'I—have things to do,' he
excused himself. But the way he said it hurt her somehow,
though she didn't know why it did.

Once inside, the little house felt different. As if the soul
had been taken out of it. Even her telephone didn't seem
to be working, she discovered, hearing only a constant
high-pitched beep when she picked it up. Neither did the

answering machine show any new messages since the last time she'd been here, which led her to suspect that the phone had been out of order for quite a while.

Frowning, she made a mental note to call the phone company to get them to see to it, as soon as she got back to the apartment. Then went off to pack for a long stay with her new lover.

Strange, she thought, even after what they'd shared, those words didn't seem real...

Giancarlo pulled up outside the small Chelsea townhouse, right on the appointed hour, and was relieved to see the door already standing open and her cases stacked neatly in the opening.

With a bit of luck, he wouldn't need to go inside. He had no wish to see inside Edward's love-nest. In fact he harboured a deep abhorrence for going near anything Edward and Natalia had shared.

As he got out of the car she appeared in the doorway. He found a smile from somewhere but it was hard. He was still involved in a struggle with himself where one part of him stubbornly justified his tactics this morning and another derided them as a man's reaction to another man pacing around his territory.

Walking across the path, he leant over to kiss her before bending to lift the cases. 'Is this it?' he asked, and noticed that she already had her coat on.

She nodded, and to his further relief stepped out behind the cases, then turned to shut the door securely before she joined him at the car.

They didn't speak as they drove away. In fact they didn't speak all the way back to his place, and the mood was heavy. He didn't like it. It worried him yet he couldn't seem to come up with anything to lighten it.

In the end he made a snap decision, and felt better for it because this was more like the man he always liked to believe he was, thinking on his feet and acting on instinct. So, instead of taking the car down to the basement, he stopped outside the front entrance.

'Stay there,' he told Natalia, then disappeared into the boot to get her luggage, took it into the foyer and told the concierge to deliver it upstairs. By the time he climbed back in the car he was beginning to feel more like himself—though he couldn't say the same for Natalia.

'What's going on?' she demanded warily.

'We're going out somewhere,' he said, gunning the engine.

'Where?' she asked.

He didn't answer simply because he had absolutely no idea other than they both needed a complete change of scenery...

They ended up in Brighton. Natalia couldn't believe it. Yet, he couldn't have come up with a better idea to help blow away the stresses and strains of the last twenty-four hours.

It was cold and the wind was sharp, and Giancarlo had to buy himself a sheepskin coat from the first shop they saw selling menswear. But they walked the beach for hours, and ate lunch in a sea-front fast-food café then walked the beach again on their way back to the car.

By the time they were driving back towards London, she'd relaxed, he'd relaxed—enough to actually look at each other without guarding their eyes.

Only once did he mention what had happened that morning, during dinner at a small restaurant they found as they hit the outskirts of London. He looked up from his plate and found her watching him. Not knowing what she was thinking tightened the muscle around his heart.

'I apologise if I—offended you this morning in the kitchen,' he said sombrely.

'Edward said you could be ruthless when you wanted to be.' She smiled a little wryly. 'I should have remembered that.'

'Edward would say that,' he returned very grimly—and changed the subject. Apology over, she noted. Time to move on and leave the rest behind.

Well, she had no argument with that—not any more anyway. It was a decision she had come to when she'd watched him drive off down the street after dropping her at home, and she'd been suddenly drenched in the terrifying idea that she was not going to see him again.

Scares like those focused the mind remarkably, she'd discovered. She had been offered the chance of a few weeks of nothing but Giancarlo. After that—nothing, no matter what else might or might not transpire.

But she was determined now to enjoy those few weeks, and not allow anything whatsoever to spoil them.

So she smiled at him across the table, then very gently asked if they needed to buy a bottle of champagne on their way home...

CHAPTER NINE

THE stock market was having a bad day. Share prices were jumping all over the place, figures flashing blue and red on the screen with no clear reason as to why they were doing it.

Sitting there, staring at the screen in front of him, Giancarlo saw nothing. His eyes were glazed. He just wasn't interested in what the world was panicking about.

For he had his very own panic button sitting not ten feet away. One quiet swing of his chair and he would be able to see her, happily getting on with her work with no idea what was going on inside his head.

Their time was up. Any day now—any moment, come to that—Natalia was going to turn to him and tell him that she was or was not carrying his baby.

Either result was going to cause problems, he knew that. But at least the former took care of itself to a certain extent. They would just have to get married. He could deal with that. Okay, so he would have to square it with Edward. Tell him the truth, and then seriously warn him off so much as remembering that Giancarlo Cardinale's new bride had once been *his* mistress.

But—*Dio*, he cursed silently, that was not a conversation he was looking forward to! He might end up killing Edward just to remove those memories from his head!

And there was Alegra to consider. What self-respecting Sicilian introduced his sister to her husband's ex-mistress? If Alegra ever discovered the truth about Natalia, she would never forgive any of them. It was in the genes.

Forgiveness was not a word a Sicilian recognised, and, although Alegra might have been living in England for the last twenty-five years of her life, she was still a Sicilian.

He would lose his sister; he didn't doubt that he would.

But even the prospect of that painful loss did not worry him as much as the prospect of a negative result to his and Natalia's wild night of unprotected sex. For—where did they go from that point on? The positive result removed the need to make choices, but the negative provided a whole new set of problems he had no answers to.

Because he didn't want to let Natalia go. Not today or next week or any week come to that—with or without their baby growing inside her. His problem here was trying to convince her of that, making *her* believe that he wanted to be with her—with or without a pregnancy.

But he had no idea if she was thinking the same thing. She was a closed book as far as her feelings for him were concerned. Oh, she loved the sex, he acknowledged cynically. He would have to be suffering from a real crisis of self-confidence if he couldn't tell that what she experienced in his bed was pretty damned special.

But was it special enough for her to want to stay with him no matter what? he pondered as he gave in to the urge to swing his chair around so he could look at her sitting there with her hair tied back in that prudish knot and wearing that skimpy red top again that did not know the meaning of the word prudish.

Did she care—really care for him?

Sensing his attention on her, she looked up and smiled. It was a smile that always made him ache. Surely no woman smiled at a man quite that way without being in love with him at least a small amount?

Who knew? He then mocked that. Remember her background. Remember Edward and what brought you here to

London in the first place. A woman with a secret lover knows how to lie with smiles, just as she knows how to lie in other ways.

Was the smile a lie?

You should detest her for what she is, a hard voice inside told him as he swung back to his busy screen again.

But he didn't detest her; he was falling in love with her. He had known that bleak fact for many days now and no amount of sensible conversation with himself was going to change that fact.

But he needed to know what it was he was dealing with and the waiting was slowly killing him...

What was he thinking while he sat there pretending to concentrate on market fluctuations when she knew he wasn't seeing a single figure flickering in front of his eyes? He was too still, too—tense, and that brief smile he'd offered her just now had been forced, Natalia was sure of it.

Was he worrying about the same thing she was worrying about? Was he sitting there wondering what the heck he was going to do if she was pregnant?

She wasn't a fool; she knew that Giancarlo was not the marrying kind. She knew he adored her body and what she could make him feel, but that didn't mean he wanted more from her than a few weeks of this sexual bliss they had managed to create for themselves. Take away the fear of an accidental baby and offer him back the life he'd had before he'd decided to play cupid for Edward and Alegra, and she was sure she would not be seeing his heels for dust as he disappeared into the sunset back to reality.

For this wasn't reality. Not for him, not for her. They'd both been living in a tightly closed cocoon in which sex was all and everything, and feelings were not so much as discussed.

Was he worried that, when it came to it, she was going to cling to him like a vine and refuse to let go? Was he worried that he was going to feel duty-bound to offer more than he wanted to give, if they discovered that she was pregnant?

Oh, please, God, she prayed fervently. Don't let me be pregnant, because I *can't* marry him. I can't stay with him beyond these next few weeks whether I am pregnant or not!

The stress in not knowing either way was beginning to get to both of them, she was acutely aware of that. So aware in fact that she didn't dare tell him that they should have known yesterday. Didn't dare think about it herself...

On a sigh Giancarlo gave up trying to appear absorbed in what he was supposed to be doing, and got up, then strolled over to brace his arms either side of her as if he were checking on what she was working on at the moment.

She smelled delicious, of something so delicate it teased his nostrils every time he came near her.

Stirred up his senses. 'How about an early lunch?' he murmured huskily, moving in to brush his mouth against her cheek.

She blushed; he felt the heat beneath his lips. It amazed him how she could still blush like that, especially after the weeks they'd spent being so intimate with each other.

Was the blush a lie too?

'You're insatiable,' she condemned him——but she didn't put up any kind of a fight as he pulled her to her feet.

'I adore you,' he replied, not even bothering any more to hold the endearments back. But then, he had stopped doing that a long time ago. She just hadn't noticed. 'Come to bed with me, *cara*,' he commanded grimly. 'I need you...'

*   *   *

I need you. Those three little words were like manna from heaven to her love-starved ears. He needed her, and when had she ever been able to deny that she needed him?

'I seem to recall you *needing* me this morning,' she reminded him as he began leading her along the hallway.

As arrogant as always, and so gorgeous it wasn't fair, 'I will take that as a challenge, *signorina*,' he warned without pausing in his stride. He trailed her behind him down the hall and across the sitting room they rarely bothered to use, into a room they used all too frequently—but she didn't demur.

For she knew she would rather be doing what they were about to do than what they had been doing, which was sitting there worrying—separately.

So, without a murmur she reclaimed her hand and took a few paces away from him. Then, with her back proudly facing him, she began to undress, coolly and unselfconsciously, aware of his eyes dark on her, and that the tension of earlier would be melting away in favour of this more appealing diversion.

So the top she was wearing came over her head, then she kicked off her shoes and shimmied out of her skirt, and, as a final touch, loosened her hair to let it flow over her shoulders before she turned to face him.

'*Dio,*' he breathed as enlightenment hit. 'You provoking little witch, you knew this was coming!'

'Homework.' She grinned, because she was wearing the red lace underwear he had bought her.

He started towards her with his fingers already at his shirt buttons and his eyes promising revenge.

But she even took control of this. 'No, I want to do that,' she said, and knocked his hands away to replace them with her own...

*   *   *

It was easy to stand here and let her undress him. It was, in fact, the easiest thing in the world for him to lose himself in the pleasurable touch of this beautiful woman as she kissed and stroked his shirt from his body, leaving him to enjoy the gentle quiver of white flesh cupped in provocative red lace as she worked her way down his torso.

He didn't touch her; he didn't attempt to help. He just stood there feeling the blood of life begin to pump the fire of passion into him as she dropped to her knees to remove his shoes and socks before reaching up to tackle his trousers.

This was what he wanted, he told himself. In fact he needed this display of sensual worship to help soothe his vulnerable ego. As he stared down at her golden head with its hot copper lights, and watched her slender white fingers efficiently strip away the rest of his clothes, he heard himself murmur lazily, 'Be gentle with me, *cara*.' Because in this game he knew exactly where he stood with her.

High on the plinth of passionate lovers—if there were such a thing.

'Why?' she questioned, looking perfectly cool as she ran her eyes over what she'd exposed. 'Nothing I see here looks that fragile.'

And to prove her claim she closed her fingers around him. The air was sucked into his lungs on a shuddering gasp that forced his eyes closed on a shaft of fierce inner response, and for a long moment he just hovered there, waiting, wanting, knowing what was coming—

Then, 'No,' he rasped on a rough-toned denial, and was suddenly pulling her to her feet so he could close his arms around her.

'Why not?' she wanted to know, and he understood her confusion, because he didn't usually stop her when she was in this kind of mood.

But he had suddenly discovered that he needed to be the one in control here. It was the only way he was going to cope with the lowering knowledge that somewhere, somehow he had become this woman's sex slave.

If anyone had told him two weeks ago that he, Giancarlo Cardinale, would one day find himself in this invidious position, he'd have laughed in their face!

The next few hours drifted by utilising the best remedy he knew for easing stress. It made for a long and languorous lunch-break. With bodies entwined they built the magic, with touch and taste and sensual caresses that helped cocoon them once again in the warm, moist-honeyed sweetness, which culminated in her lying beneath him. Limbs wrapped with limbs, and with him moving deep inside her, with his eyes and his mouth and the gentle touch of his hands, he made a different kind of love to her.

It was a small piece of heaven.

The same remedy came into play again late that same evening. And another day went by, and another, until nothing was easing his stress levels—because she still wasn't telling him anything he needed to know.

Unable to stand it any longer, he took a different kind of evasive action.

'Go and get dressed up,' he said one evening. 'We are eating somewhere special tonight...'

There was nothing that unusual in them eating out—they ate out quite frequently, in fact. So what felt different about this evening? she asked herself while her fingers scrambled through her jewellery case in search of her watch, which she had mislaid somewhere.

A sign of distraction in anyone's book, she mused, feeling Giancarlo's eyes lazily watching her as he lounged on the bed, dressed and ready to go and just waiting for her to finish getting ready.

It was what he was wearing that was making tonight different, she admitted. The black dinner suit and bow-tie turned him into a different person—a hard, sharp, breath-catchingly sophisticated person she felt very much out of her depth with.

'Have you seen my watch?' she asked, trying to sound perfectly normal when in actual fact she was feeling quite strange beneath the wrap she had tied loosely round her.

'What does this look like?' he murmured teasingly, reaching into the case to slide a slender wrist-watch out from beneath a thin red silk handkerchief it had been hiding beneath.

'Oh...' she gasped...

The strangled little sound sharpened his interest, sending his lazy gaze off to check what it was he was holding casually between finger and thumb—and felt himself floundering on the rocks of a mind-sizzling fury.

'It—it's very old,' she told him shakily, trying for a dry little laugh that didn't quite make it. 'It doesn't even work. It-it's an heirloom of m-my great-grandmother's.'

'*Your* great-grandmother?' he repeated, waiting with gritted teeth for her confirming nod. It came, and his inner anger soared to a place it had never visited before.

For he knew this watch. He had even been allowed to handle it very carefully once when Edward had shown it to him years ago—and explained to him that the delicately worked, enamelled diamond-set cabochon wrist-watch had belonged to *Edward's* grandmother! It was the only thing of value she had managed to bring with her to England after the fall of Imperial Russia.

And it was a genuine Fabergé, unique and priceless. 'For

my first-born great-granddaughter,' she had instructed her grandson.

Giancarlo felt as if his skin were being lifted off his flesh by a rash of fury. For in the face of never producing a grandchild of either sex with the death of Marco, Edward, it seemed, had decided to pass the watch on to his mistress! Not even his wife of twenty-five loyal, faithful years—but his bloody mistress!

And she keeps it stuffed in a box with a load of worthless trinkets, he then added contemptuously. What does that say about the real person she is? he asked himself. If it means so little to her, then why the hell hasn't she sold it and made herself a tidy profit out of Edward's love?

'I'll have it fixed for you,' he offered.

'No!' she almost shrieked in her urgency. Then tried to calm herself. 'I t-tried once, but they said it w-would cost too m-much.'

I just bet they did, he thought grimly as he sent her horror leaping when he casually flipped the watch into his pocket. 'Let me try,' he offered. 'I know someone who takes great delight in restoring old watches...'

'I'd rather keep it exactly as it is,' she said, needing to moisten her lips as she held out her hand. 'In f-fact it means too much to me to w-want to risk letting it out of my sight.'

'I'm not going to lose it for you,' he assured. 'Just get it—'

'No, Giancarlo!' she snapped—in more ways than vocally, he noted cynically as she made a sudden dive towards his pocket in her desperation to get the watch back! 'Give it to me! Please—!'

His response was to lift her up by the waist and drop her down on the bed, then to follow her. 'Make me,' he taunted, feeling anger flip him over into some other place entirely that literally set his teeth on edge. His eyes were hot, his body hard and—God help him, but he wanted her!

Wanted her so badly that it took him by storm.

His only consolation to that, he supposed later when he stood beneath the ice-cold jet of the shower, was that she had been affected as badly as he.

But when he came back into the bedroom, he found his clothes waiting for him on the neatly remade bed—and the watch was no longer in his pocket...

Natalia didn't know why he had brought them here. Glancing around her, she tried very hard to see what the attraction was in the most fashionable and therefore busiest restaurant in London right now.

After the small, more intimate places he had taken her to before, this place felt brash and noisy and over the top with its trendy decor and its trendy people all greeting each other with trendy kisses wrapped up in super-trendy smiles.

Why? she wanted to know. What is supposed to be so different about tonight, that he decided to bring me to a place like this?

You know why, the mocking little answer came back, sending her stress levels inching up another couple of notches. The man is straining at the leash with boredom while he waits to find out if he's going to be let off the hook by you.

Suddenly she wanted to be sick...

If she got any paler she would probably pass out! Giancarlo thought grimly as he fielded yet another greeting from someone whose name he didn't even remember.

They ate fashionable food from fashionable plates, with London's fashionable set milling all around them, and he hated every minute of it even while he kept his social smile in place, and pretended this was just what he wanted.

But it wasn't. Hell—he didn't know what he wanted any more! She tied him in knots, he admitted, glaring at her sitting there across the table from him looking so damn beautiful in her sparkling black dress that made him think of the black underwear she was probably wearing, and with her hair like silk against her shoulders—and that cheap gold watch, which reminded him of another watch, circling her slender wrist.

And he didn't like the way other men were eyeing her up, he added to his list of grievances, though she didn't seem to notice, he had to confess.

In fact, she couldn't look more unimpressed with a place if she tried to be!

Or maybe it was him she was unimpressed with, he pondered with a sting that made him snatch up his wine-glass. Did the urbane sophisticate in the bow-tie and the dinner suit, who drew the flattering attention of all the other sophisticates here, not reach her at all?

When was she going to give him the answer? he added on a restless shrug of his black-silk-covered shoulders that showed how Natalia Deyton was beginning to get under his skin in more ways than he wanted to deal with! She gave him nothing and he gave everything! he decided with an arrogance that tried to completely ignore that what he was getting from her was exactly what he'd aimed for!

Edward's mistress becoming *his* mistress. Nothing more, nothing less.

On paper he supposed he was a step or two up from a man who was twice her age and married with it, he allowed with a bitter kind of wit.

Though even he couldn't afford to give out Fabergé heirlooms as payment for services rendered! And—hell, he grimly extended on that theme. If he—Giancarlo—had found it easy enough to take her from Edward, then what was to stop her moving on as easily if a bigger catch came along?

An answer to one specific question, he reminded himself with a burning flash of his eyes in her direction. Yes or no, Natalia? he questioned silently. Surely she had to know something by now…?

He wanted out, she just knew he did. He was feeling so trapped by their situation that he was barely managing to contain his frustration with it any longer. She was going to have to let him off the hook. Yes or no to the question that was burning holes in both their heads. She was going to have to set him free, then disappear. It was the only thing for her to do even if the very idea was making her feel positively nauseous…

Why was she looking so down in the mouth and wan-faced? Giancarlo thought bitterly. As long as she had him over a barrel, she was sitting pretty!

Then it happened. No hint, no warning. She was just coming to her feet with some murmured excuse about going to the cloakroom, then she swayed and her eyes closed, and he saw her face turn deathly pale as her legs began to go from under her.

He was there to catch her. Anger forgotten, frustrations, resentments—everything sluiced away in that single swift move of his body from his chair to her side so he could take her weight for her.

'Okay?' he asked roughly.

'Yes,' she breathed, but he knew she wasn't. He could feel her trembling, and she was having to fight the need to lean heavily on him. 'Do you think we can go now?' she begged shakily.

'Of course.' Without another word, he carefully fed her slender frame beneath his shoulder and began carefully guiding her between tables with curious eyes following them...

Natalia couldn't really blame them for their curiosity. Giancarlo was holding her so close that she was finding it difficult to put one foot in front of the other. He continued to hold her like that while he paid the bill, and only released her for as long as it took to help her into her coat. Then she was back beneath the protection of his arm before she had a chance to move a single step.

'You can let go of me now,' she told him when they eventually made it outside.

'No,' he replied, that was all. It was gruff and it was tight and it declared no room for argument as he herded her down the street to the nearest taxi rank, and helped her inside a black cab.

She wasn't sure why they had come by taxi tonight, unless it had something to do with the amount of wine Giancarlo had drunk through dinner. She had a horrible feeling he had come out with the specific intention of getting himself drunk. And his mood had been so short and surly she hadn't known quite how to deal with it.

It didn't help that she had been feeling under the weather for most of the evening—ever since he'd noticed her watch, in fact.

No, don't think about that, she told herself with a small shudder.

The shudder made him turn his head to glance at her sharply. 'I'm okay,' she assured him, but it wasn't the truth.

She felt weak and dizzy, and she knew she should have said something sooner. Her own quiet mood had affected his mood. But she had been worried and frightened of saying anything in case it forced the whole wretched problem right out in the open.

Now the problem didn't need forcing out, because it was sitting here between them like a great lump of rock just waiting to be shattered by one tiny comment—I think I'm pregnant. Or—I think you are pregnant, depending on which one of them decided to say it first.

Yet neither of them said a single word all the way back to the apartment. He was grim-faced and withdrawn and she felt her heart sting every time she dared a quick glance at his profile. Handsome didn't even begin to cover what made Giancarlo Cardinale the compelling force he was to her. She adored every lean, hard, noble feature, every flicker of his lashes, every twitch of his flat-lined, sensually moulded mouth. She even adored the way he was being very careful to keep his eyes away from her eyes because it showed that he was as aware as she was that the moment of truth was too close for comfort.

And she adored the way his hand was gripping her hand so tightly, even over that imaginary lump of rock which had trouble stamped all over it...

He couldn't say a word. He didn't dare. Not until he'd had time to think—though what that meant he had been doing for the last few weeks made it anybody's guess, he grimly admitted. Because *this* was thinking, which just went to show how suspicion could fool you where reality could not.

'*Incinta...*' he murmured, feeling a whole new set of powerful emotions grab a tight hold of him by the sheer weight of her condition.

'What?' Natalia prompted.

'Nothing,' he said, not realising he'd spoken out loud, and glad she didn't understand his language.

The taxi drew up outside the apartment then, saving either of them the need to speak again while he paid the driver and climbed out himself before helping Natalia down onto the path beside him.

She still looked pale, and her hand gripped his arm with enough force to tell him that she still felt frail. Without a word he folded her back beneath his arm to take her into the building. The concierge was there, they all smiled politely at each other, and the lift waited at the ready to transport them into privacy.

He needed that, he acknowledged. Privacy to think with this brand-new clarity of mind he was now experiencing.

Keeping her close to him while he activated the lift, he then spent the time it took to reach their floor in silent communion with the top of her head, thinking, feeling— *Dio*, feeling more than he could actually believe was possible just because one small suspicion had become hard fact...

God, she felt awful. Sick in the stomach and light in the head. If he didn't say something she was going to start crying! She just knew she was because, if it wasn't enough that his silence was killing her, then this gentle, protective way he was treating her was enough to make the tears flow.

Did he have to crowd her into the corner like this? she thought on a sudden bout of breathlessness that had her sinking back further into the lift corner. He was all brawn and bone and familiar scents that were beginning to make her feel really dizzy.

'*Stai bene?*' he enquired, clearly sensing something.

'What's happened to your English?' she snapped at him in an effort to dispel whatever it was that was happening to her.

'It is here,' he replied, as calm as anything.

'Then try using it if you want to be understood,' she advised, sounding waspish but not even caring any more. The lift doors opened then. Maybe it was timely, because she'd seen the way his chest had lifted and fallen. He was controlling the desire to retaliate in kind.

Aware that she was stupidly treading the fine line to destruction, she slipped out from beneath his overpowering stance and walked quickly out of the lift and across the lobby on legs that were threatening to collapse—

The telephone was ringing. She stopped and frowned as she turned instinctively in the direction of the nearest extension which happened to be in the office.

'I will get it,' he said, striding towards the office. She didn't demur, for it had to be for him. The life of a venture capitalist didn't recognise time zones.

She was just removing her coat when she heard his voice make its usual deep curt acknowledgement to whoever was trying to contact him.

Silence followed. Something about it made her go still. Then his voice came, hard and tight, and as she stared at him he spun his back to her, his body bristling with tension as he became involved in a question and answer session in thick deep Italian with whoever was on the other end of the phone.

Then the phone was slammed down. Silence hit. For the space of ten excruciating seconds, he just continued to stand there staring at the wall in front of him while she waited with bated breath, somehow knowing that something dreadful had just happened.

When he did move, she found herself taking an unsteady

step backwards as he strode towards her. 'W-what's wrong?' she asked anxiously.

'Nothing,' he clipped, but he was lying. 'I have to go out,' he announced, striding right by her. Then he was gone, disappearing back into the lift and sending it downwards without even offering her a single glance!

Whomever he had been talking to had given him an excuse to get away from here before they had a chance to talk—and, good grief, but he'd taken it with wings on his feet!

It hurt. She couldn't pretend it didn't. In a daze filled with bitter new experiences tonight, she walked into the office, draped her coat over a chair, then sat down without really knowing she had done it.

A flickering red light suddenly intruded on the edge of her vision. As she turned towards it, it was purely instinctive to press the play-back button on the answering machine.

Almost immediately a shrill, near-hysterical voice came whipping into the room with her. And even though it spoke in an agitated mix of Italian and English, she got the drift of what it was saying.

'Where are you, Giancarlo?' it was demanding urgently. 'I have been ringing and ringing—' It was his sister's voice, Natalia realised as Alegra suddenly switched to Italian. She recognised it because she had spoken to her several times while working with Edward.

Then—'Edward.' She picked out his name from the garble. Followed almost instantly by another couple of recognisable words that had her going cold inside.

It was the link between Edward and the name of a famous hospital right here in London that really shook her.

Edward was ill. She knew it without a hint of a doubt in her head!

Natalia got up and ran...

CHAPTER TEN

GIANCARLO felt sick. Standing here with Alegra weeping in his arms and talking wildly, all he could think was—I am going to be sick.

'He made the confession, Giancarlo,' Alegra sobbed out in shrill broken English. 'He starts acting strange. Then he suddenly insists we leave the cruise and fly home. We are almost here when he has the attack. He thinks he is going to die, so he decides to tell all! But what does this confession do for me?' she choked, so utterly distraught it was wretched. 'He took another woman to his bed! He made a child with her! He betrayed me and defiled me and now he is going to die on me!'

'He will not die, *cara*,' he murmured, finding the comforting words from somewhere, but he didn't know where from because his brain had crashed, the sheer scale of the horror unfolding before him just too much for it to take in. 'Shh,' he soothed. 'He will live—he will live.'

And he *will*, Giancarlo found himself vowing angrily. Because he wanted Edward very much alive so he could personally kill both him and Natalia Deyton!

Natalia. His heart suddenly wrenched, the pain and the anger shooting out in all directions and holding him stock-stone still. Natalia the witch. Natalia the bitch. Natalia the lying, cheating, artful deceiver, who had knowingly and calculatingly lured him into bed with her—so she could foist Edward's bastard off on him!

'But then he deserves to die for doing this to me!'

153

Alegra burst out. 'A child, Giancarlo! He made a child with another woman! I will never forgive him!'

The Sicilian promise. His bones clenched at the sound of it. Yet he understood it—hell, did he understand!

A sound by the waiting-room door caught his attention. Looking up, he immediately began to burn inside because—there she was, standing in the doorway as if his own wrath had conjured her up, and looking achingly, destructively beautiful in her sparkling black dress, which somehow reminded him of the Fabergé watch.

A watch she'd probably filched out of Edward's safe along with everything else he'd asked her to get out of there. As her own idea of payment for services rendered—to both Edward and himself?

And now she had the cheek to turn up here, when she must know that the game was up, looking all pale and ethereal and—

Dio! 'I am going to make you pay for this,' he hissed at her his own Sicilian promise from between tightly gritted teeth.

She blinked as if he'd slapped her. Yet the very idea of laying another finger on her traitorous flesh had his stomach reeling all over again. At the same dizzying moment his sister broke free from his arms and saw her standing there.

'It is she!' Alegra exclaimed shrilly. 'She is the one, Giancarlo—she is the one! I know the hair, I know the eyes!'

'Edward...' Natalia whispered shakily. 'H-how is he? What—?'

'Get out!' Giancarlo blasted at her, losing touch with himself as the sound of Edward's name quivering on her lips sent a shaft of burning black anguish thrusting its way through him. 'You are not wanted here. Get out of my sight!'

Now she had gone as white as a sheet, he saw. Her beautiful eyes so dark, it could be anguish colouring them like that. But it was not anguish. It was the look of horror at being found out!

'I just need to know how he is,' she insisted. 'I d-don't want to make trouble, b-but I must know if he—'

'You are the trouble!' his sister fiercely responded, diverting Natalia's attention away from him...

Natalia saw the other woman start towards her with her eyes spitting out the kind of hatred and venom Edward had always predicted she would see.

'Edward would not be in here if it was not for you!' Alegra cried. 'You could not leave well alone! You had to seek him out and play on his broken heart!'

'He loves me,' Natalia whispered in her own defence. 'Love doesn't break hearts, it helps to heal—'

Derision lanced across Giancarlo's hard face, and his sister almost jumped on her in her rage. 'How dare you say that when it is you who has poisoned his mind?' the older woman launched at her shrilly. 'You put yourself in my dead son's place and fed on Edward's grief and pain until he could bear it no longer and made himself ill!'

Alegra lifted up a hand. Thinking she was about to be attacked, Natalia stiffened up warily, her eyes blinking in rapid confusion as another, larger hand appeared in her vision, also raised as if ready to strike. But all Giancarlo did was capture his sister's hand before it could throw the expected blow.

After that Natalia just stood there shaking with shock and pain, feeling as if she was being bombarded by hatred from two different sources. With Alegra it was with the words that were still spilling from her lips. With Giancarlo it was simply in his expression.

And Edward was right, she realised painfully. These people did not know the meaning of compassion.

Edward. Her heart lurched. 'Will one of you please tell me how he is?' she begged anxiously.

'Why do you want to know?' Giancarlo jeered at her. 'So you can make a judgement whether it is worth foisting his baby back on to him now that I know the truth about you?'

The truth? Her mouth went slack in disbelief. Was he saying what she thought he was saying here? Was he actually daring to suggest that any baby she might be carrying belonged to *Edward*?

Oh, God—the nausea came back with a vengeance when she began to really understand what it was that Giancarlo was thinking here. 'You believe I was Edward's mistress.' She breathed the terrible words out loud. He flinched as if she'd hit him. She wished she had done. 'You think I was trying to foist his baby onto you!'

'The truth always sounds shocking when spoken out loud,' he grated.

'*Your* truth, yes,' she agreed.

'What are you talking about, Giancarlo?' his sister put in bewilderedly.

He didn't even hear her, he was so busy despising Natalia. 'Oh, stop looking so damned bewildered!' he bit out in disgust. 'Edward has already confessed everything in sheer fear of dying with it all still festering on his soul!'

'Stop it!' his sister cried. 'Stop it, the both of you. This is wrong. It is—'

'The only person with a guilty conscience around here should be you for daring to believe such a filthy thing about either of us!' Natalia sliced over the top of her.

'Edward always said you came from crude stock,' she told him, taking great pleasure from seeing his arrogant face turn to rock. 'He was right! You couldn't have a more primitive view of life if you tried!'

'And trying to foist one man's child off on his brother-in-law is not crude?'

'Giancarlo!' Alegra inserted furiously. 'This has gone far enough!'

More than far enough, agreed Natalia, and with a final slaying glance at him she turned and walked out to go in search of the one who really mattered here.

Edward, leaving Edward's wife to put her brother's vile misconceptions in order. She even smiled in cold satisfaction as she heard the beginning of it before the door closed behind her.

'She is not the woman Edward betrayed me with!' Alegra was saying furiously. 'She is the *child* his betrayal spawned, you fool...!'

Giancarlo caught up with Natalia just as she was leaning over a distraught Edward and trying to calm him down. 'Shh,' she was soothing him—just as Giancarlo had been soothing Alegra not so long ago. 'Please, darling, don't do this, you're going to make yourself worse!'

But Edward wouldn't be soothed. 'I couldn't find you anywhere. I tried your house, the office, I even tried Giancarlo! But he said he'd sent you away on a fact-finding mission to Fillens in Manchester, and I believed him!' he choked out in self-disgust. 'I actually believed him and put you aside to worry about Alegra and myself instead.'

'As you should have done,' Natalia attempted to console him.

'No, I shouldn't,' Edward groaned. 'I should have

smelled a rat from the moment he said it! But it took me
two whole weeks before it suddenly hit me—in Nassau of
all the places—that there was no way he would send you
anywhere like that unless he had an ulterior motive for
doing so!'

'Shh,' she tried again.

'So I rang the firm,' Edward continued hoarsely. 'Got
Howard Fiske who'd apparently not long come back from
Milan. The swine was more than happy to tell me that
you'd moved in with my brother-in-law within days of him
arriving. And that's when it really hit!' he gasped out.
'Why Giancarlo had arranged the cruise and put himself
in my place here in London. He must have found out about
you and was doing the typical Sicilian thing by taking
revenge for *my* sin out on you!'

'You mean—he came here to deliberately seduce me?'
Natalia said, while Giancarlo stood there unnoticed, feeling
the full weight of his own culpability land squarely upon
his own rigid shoulders.

'Natalia…' he murmured, unable to remain quiet any
longer.

She turned towards him, and for the first time Giancarlo
looked into her eyes and saw Edward's eyes looking accusingly back at him. He looked at her hair and saw the
colour Edward's hair used to be before the silver had over-
run the gold. His stomach contracted, for what he was
seeing was a terrible truth that had been staring him in the
face from the very beginning, but he had been too blinded
by prejudice to see it.

Sexual prejudice, he expanded sombrely.

Sex probably covered his blindness very well—in the
beginning at any rate. He had wanted Natalia Deyton so
badly from the first moment he'd looked into those eyes
that to see then what he should have seen would have

stopped his plans of seduction dead in their tracks. So he hadn't let himself see. For how did a Sicilian male seduce the daughter of one of his own family members? He didn't. It was as simple and neat as that.

And it was quite monstrous to know how low he had trodden in his *want* for Edward's beautiful daughter.

'You stay away from her!' Edward clearly held the same bitter belief. 'You've had your revenge, now get the hell away from both of us!'

It was the ugly scene in the waiting room playing itself out in reverse, Giancarlo noted. And he quietly tried again. 'Natalia—'

'Just go,' she cut in, having to use both hands to keep her father from getting up off the bed in his weak effort to protect her. 'You are making him worse.'

Could it get any worse? 'We need to talk,' he insisted, and saw by the sudden darkening of her eyes that she would rather slay him than speak to him. His grimace acknowledged her right to think like that—but he didn't back down. 'Talk,' he repeated warningly, and, with a final glance at Edward's angry struggle, he turned and walked away, taking the sight of Natalia's tears right along with him...

'He hurt you, didn't he?' Edward had seen the tears too. 'I'll never forgive him.'

'Nor will I,' Natalia agreed, but had to wonder why that knowledge wounded her so much.

You know why, she then mocked herself. Because you love him, cruel, hard, ruthless man that he is. 'Please stop fighting me, Edward,' she pleaded. 'Do you want me to lose you along with everything else?'

'I'm all right,' he snapped out impatiently. 'It was just

a little panic attack during the flight, that was all. Nothing worthy of all this fuss!'

He should have said heart attack but Natalia didn't correct him, because he was probably half right, and panic was what had helped bring it on in the first place.

'What did he do to you?' he muttered, falling back in frustration because he was too weak to even throw off a lightweight like Natalia.

'He thought I was your mistress,' she said, then smiled at her father's shocked expression because he just hadn't realised the twisted view others had had of their little deception.

After that she told him everything, quietly and unemotionally because there had been enough of that expended tonight. And also because the truth needed to be told from all angles if this muddled situation was ever to be sorted out.

But, 'God, I'm going to kill him!' Edward rasped when she withered to an empty finish, and he started trying to get up again.

'You will do nothing of the kind, you stupid—stupid man!' another angry voice commanded. 'Not when *you* are the one to blame for all of this!'

It was Alegra. Instantly placed on the wary defensive, Natalia straightened stiffly away from him while Edward sank with a groan back against the pillows.

'If you've come here to continue your family vendetta then you can turn about and leave again,' Edward grimly informed his wife of twenty-five years.

'I have not come to do anything,' Alegra replied haughtily, 'but be formally introduced to your daughter.'

Looking at her standing there, a diminutive figure dressed in blue, who held herself with a pride which gave her stature, Natalia had to admire just what it must be costing Alegra Knight to say that. And for a moment—just a moment—she saw Alegra's resemblance to her brother, the same arrogant tilt to her head, the same darkly challenging eyes, the same—

No. She shook the comparison away, not wanting to think about Giancarlo right now.

'Not if you're going to start spitting out insults again,' Edward refused harshly.

The eyes flashed once more, Natalia thought of Giancarlo again—and again she thrust the comparison away. 'The only person in this room who deserves insulting is you,' Alegra hit back. 'So you may climb out of that defensive hole you are trying to hide in and behave like the gentleman I used to think you!'

To Natalia's surprise, Edward smiled—albeit wryly. 'You have the silken tongue of a Sicilian asp,' he dryly informed his wife.

'I have the power to bite like one also,' Alegra returned.

And suddenly Natalia was beginning to feel definitely in the way as something she had never been privy to before began to fill the air space.

It was love. It was affection. Despite all the lies and pain and anger, it was a deep and abiding togetherness nurtured through years and years of tender loving care administered from one constant soul to another.

Bearing witness to it brought the tears back to Natalia's eyes because this was exactly what her father had been protecting when he'd kept her a secret from everyone. Now the secret was out, and she was afraid it was going to spoil everything he had worked so hard to hold on to.

'I have been sent to instruct you that it is time to rest,' his wife firmly changed the subject. 'So make these introductions so we two can go away and leave you to recover from your sinful life.'

'I've told you before,' Edward said harshly. 'Natalia was born *before* I married you!'

'Two months?'

Natalia winced, understanding the curt thrust. So did her father, who became very weary suddenly. And for her the tears became harder to fight, because in the end, and once Alegra had time to think it all over properly, the fact that Edward had married her instead of standing by his ex-lover and child said a lot about his love for Alegra.

A nurse arrived then, insisting they leave now, and a few minutes later Natalia found herself outside in the corridor with her father's wife.

'Don't weep, child,' Alegra Knight murmured, and a gentle hand came to rest on her shoulder. 'We fight. It means nothing. We know that, even if you do not.'

'I never wanted to come between you,' she whispered painfully. 'I j-just needed to know him. It was...'

'I know.' The gentle hand squeezed her into a thickened silence. 'Edward has explained all. You do not need to justify yourself to me—or to anyone else concerned here, come to that,' she added carefully.

'He was never unfaithful to you after you married,' Natalia felt compelled to say. 'He never saw either me or my mother again, from the day I was born. If I've forgiven him for all the years of rejection, can't you forgive him too?'

The hand was removed. Alegra began walking. 'He was unfaithful during our betrothal,' she said coldly. 'Would you find it easy to forgive that?'

No, she wouldn't, Natalia had to admit.

'And while I was busy grieving the death of our beloved son, he was discovering he had another child to help salve his broken heart.'

'I didn't know about Marco until after Edward and I

met, or I wouldn't...' Her voice trailed away on a guilty thickening of her throat, which required her to swallow before she could try again. 'M-my mother had passed away, you see, and I found all these private papers relating to a father I never knew existed. It...'

This time she really couldn't go on. It had been one of the lowest points in all her life to discover that the mother she had adored had lied when she'd told her that her father was dead. Twenty-four relatively happy years suddenly soured on a medley of remembered conversations about a man called Nathaniel Deyton, a merchant seaman with eyes and hair the same colour as her own, who'd had the chance to meet his baby girl only once before the sea had taken him. There had never been such a person as Nathaniel Deyton. It was a name her mother had made up and taken up when she'd moved out of London with her daughter, to live the rest of her life in a quiet little village in Suffolk where nobody knew her so could not dispute her story.

From the moment Natalia had found out about her real father, she had made it an obsession to trace him and try to get to know him. It had taken several months to locate the right Edward Knight. Yet it had taken him mere days to reply to her tentative letter of introduction. They'd met in a crowded wine bar not far from his office building, and in minutes had been so at peace with each other that it seemed strange now to look back and know that first meeting had been only six months ago.

'He gave you the Fabergé watch, didn't he?'

Pulling herself back to the present, Natalia sucked in a thick breath of air and nodded. 'If you want it back, I'll be very happy to—'

'No, I was not asking for it,' Alegra responded. 'It belongs to you. You had a right to receive it. I just—missed it, that was all, several months ago, and Edward refused to say what he had done with it. So I began to worry—as wives do—whether he had found some other woman he preferred to give it to.'

'So you mentioned as much to Giancarlo,' Natalia murmured, beginning to see a whole new way of looking at the scene she and Giancarlo had had about the watch.

'But it was Howard Fiske who gave the silly imaginings of a grieving woman their hard substance,' Alegra added. 'He rang Giancarlo in Milan and voiced his—suspicions about your relationship with Edward. Giancarlo being Giancarlo—' she shrugged with true Sicilian understanding '—decided to put a stop to it before I had to find out.'

And the rest, as they said, was history, Natalia soberly concluded. 'He deliberately set out to use me.'

Alegra stopped walking. So did Natalia. They had almost reached the main foyer but neither seemed to notice. 'You need to talk to him about that,' she advised, and at the sudden freeze she saw encase Natalia's face she sighed and said, 'I am going back to sit with Edward, for I cannot leave here until I know the danger has surely passed.'

'Do you want me to stay with you?' It was instant and instinctive to make the offer.

But Alegra's refusal made its point. 'We need time alone together. And I need time to get used to the idea of you being a part of my family now.' A brief smile tried to take the sting out of her words.

Natalia smiled back in an effort to make it known that she understood, even if it did hurt. Maybe Alegra saw the hurt, because her cold expression softened a little. 'Go now,' she advised. 'I will find you if I need to but I do not see this problem he has caused his silly heart worsening now that the truth is out in the open.'

No, Natalia thought wearily. Neither did she. Edward

had been living under a terrible strain for the last year one way or another. It was no wonder his heart had finally insisted he give himself a break.

About to turn away, Alegra spoke again. 'Please forgive my rudeness to you before,' she intoned. 'It was a shock when he suddenly collapsed then began to confess all to me.'

'I'm sorry you had to find out that way,' Natalia responded, not knowing what else to say to make any of this better.

Alegra just smiled another of those smiles, then turned to walk back the way she had come, leaving Natalia standing there watching her go with tears in her eyes again, though she couldn't decide who they were for—herself or Alegra.

The whole situation had always had the potential to turn ugly. Now it had done, she found herself half wishing she had never contacted Edward, then there would have been none of this. No secret, no lies—and no ruthless Sicilian hell bent on waging a vendetta.

'Are you ready to leave now?' an all-too-familiar voice enquired.

A wave of pain washed over her, turning her around before she had a chance to think. Giancarlo was standing not three feet away. Big, dark, and with no expression whatsoever showing on his lean face.

She wanted to turn away again but found she couldn't. She wanted to hate him but found she couldn't even do that. So she ended up just standing there hurting all over, which made such a terrible mockery of everything...

She didn't know whether to hit him or hug him. Her mouth was vulnerable but her eyes were like glass, a dark grey glass with the blue lost behind a film of tears which, even as he looked sombrely into them, was quickly frosting into ice to shut him out.

But the quivering mouth was letting her down. She was hurting and she desperately needed someone to hold her right now.

Dio, he thought, so did he. But touching, he knew, was out of the question. Touch her now and she would probably never forgive him for violating that invisible barrier of self-defence she was standing beyond.

'I have a taxi waiting outside,' he told her, and was relieved to hear the words come out level because he certainly wasn't feeling level inside.

He expected the mute shake of her head in refusal. He even expected the cold shoulder she offered him as she altered direction so that she could walk by him without offering him a single word.

He didn't try to stop her, but as she went by him he fed quietly after her, 'I was deceived as much as you were.'

The claim stopped her, but she didn't turn, and his throat grew tight as he stood watching her hair and her dress glitter in the overhead lights of the foyer.

'No,' she said, that was all, just that small, tight denial, then she was walking again, beautiful head held high, slender spine as straight as an arrow, sensational legs long in their stride.

Grimly determined, he followed, drawing level with her, then adjusting his stride to hers. The gap between them was still there—not quite as wide but wide enough for her to feel her defensive barrier was not being breached. Neither did she turn to look at him and he did not look at her. The exit doors were automatic, swinging smoothly open as they reached them and they stepped out into the cold night air. She paused and shivered, her hands going up to cup her bare arms.

'Where is your coat?' he asked, beckoning the private taxi forward.

'I forgot it.'

He grimaced because he hadn't expected her to reply. The taxi drew up. It was a top-of-the-range black Mercedes promising warmth and comfort—if he could get her inside it.

Ignoring the car, she began searching the street for the nearest taxi rank.

'Money?' he prompted next.

She indicated with a shrug of one folded arm the sparkling black evening bag dangling from her wrist by its narrow strap.

It was communication of sorts, he supposed. 'Enough to take you to Chelsea—after midnight—when taxi fares go through the roof?'

The flicker of her lashes told him he'd hit the right button to achieve his aims. And, as if on cue, the driver stepped out of the Mercedes and jumped to open the rear door for them. Silently, Giancarlo thanked him for his perfect timing.

'Come on,' he invited. 'I will take you home.'

'My home,' she said, swinging her head round to look directly at him at last.

His hands twitched at his sides with a need to just grab her and kiss some healthy life back into her. But the frost went too deep and it might ruin his chances completely. 'If that is what you want,' he therefore agreed.

'It is,' she confirmed and without another word she stepped forward and slid into the back of the Mercedes.

With a grim nod of his head at the driver, he closed her inside, then he walked around to the other side of the car to get in as the driver sat behind his wall of tinted glass.

They moved away from the kerb with Natalia staring

fixedly out of her window and Giancarlo gauging that he had about five minutes before she began to realise she wasn't going to Chelsea.

'A Russian great-grandmother,' he remarked. 'Now I know where all the fire and the passion comes from.'

Her head flicked round, and it was as if a light had suddenly been switched on inside her. 'Don't you dare comment on my background!' she threw at him hotly. 'Don't you even so much as dare to make it any business of yours!'

'It is my business if you are sharing your genes with my baby,' he pointed out, quite happily fanning the flames.

'I am not pregnant!' she flashed.

'You cannot know that with such certainty,' he replied.

'Tomorrow will tell,' she muttered, and turned away again.

'Why tomorrow specifically?' he asked curiously, following every flash and restless quiver she made and loving every one of them because it meant he was beginning to melt the ice. Once the ice was gone he could begin dealing with the melting woman. A woman who was in for a big fight if she was foolishly allowing herself to believe that he was going to let go of her now.

Because he wasn't.

'I'll buy one of those test-kit things,' she informed him. 'First thing in the morning.'

'Good idea,' he said agreeably. 'We will watch the result with interest—together—'

'You won't be there to watch it!' she flung at him.

The caution brought her eyes back into contact with his—and this time he held on to them by sheer grim resolve. 'Oh, yes, I will,' he countered very seriously. 'For I do not think I should trust you to tell me the truth, you see...'

CHAPTER ELEVEN

IT WAS like waving a red rag to a bull, especially when Natalia had been intending to do just that if necessary and lie to Giancarlo! 'Will you want a DNA test done as well, if I find I am pregnant?' she enquired ever so, ever so acidly.

The dark eyes flickered, though they didn't release her eyes. 'Do you think it could be a possibility that such a test may be required?' he countered.

It was a clean hit. Natalia even found herself acknowledging it with a gasp, because she knew she had set herself up for that. They had known each other for a few weeks only. Not long enough to cover a full menstrual cycle, in fact. So even with his rotten suspicions about her relationship with Edward out of the way, she could quite easily be pregnant by some other imaginary guy, she supposed. How would he know that she hadn't been involved in an intimate relationship with any man for years?

She had been too involved in other things, such as a mother dying, and a newly found father to pour all her emotions into.

'No, a DNA test won't be needed,' she replied, resenting having to say it at all. Then she wrenched her eyes away to glare out of the side window while she waited for him to come back with some cynically disbelieving reply.

And why not? she asked herself bitterly. You fell into his bed like a woman who did that kind of thing all the time! Shame engulfed her, followed by a real contempt for the person she had allowed herself to become in her reckless desire for this man.

Then she stopped thinking. Her eyes blinked into focus on what it was she was actually glaring at. 'We're going the wrong way,' she announced, and was already leaning forward to knock on the glass partition so she could tell the driver—when another hand closed around her hand.

Suddenly the sparks were flying, crackling around the inner compartment and bouncing off all surfaces in a skin-against-skin chemical reaction that rendered her totally breathless.

Unable to stop herself, she glanced at him and felt her heart begin to race when she saw what was written in his eyes. He was going to kiss her—and she didn't want him to!—yet her eyes dropped to his mouth of their own hungry volition. It began to move, her throat locked, her own lips beginning to heat in preparation for what was about to come to them.

'Keys,' he said.

Lost in a daze of her own making, 'What?' she said.

'The keys to your Chelsea house,' he gently extended. 'Do you have them with you in that small bag?'

Natalia felt herself deflate like a popped balloon as reality pierced sheer fantasy. 'No,' she breathed.

Having made his point, Giancarlo let go of her hand, leaving her to complete the deflation by sinking shakily back into the soft luxury of leather, knowing now that, whatever else had been killed between them, the sex was still there, simmering quietly in the background waiting for its usual release.

'I'll just pick up my keys and go.' She seemed to feel it necessary to state her intentions.

He didn't even bother to reply, which to her stated *his* intentions far more ominously than an outright denial could have done. He had coerced her into getting into this car with him because he had been gunning for a complete showdown tonight even though he must know that it wouldn't be fair.

Not after the evening she had just been put through. Not after what she'd found out and hadn't had time yet to decide what she really felt about it all.

Yet she didn't persist with the point, and she didn't understand *why* she didn't. Which had her finishing the rest of the journey with the feeling of being trapped by herself as much as him.

The car stopped; the driver jumped out to open her door for her while Giancarlo got out on the other side. With a polite thanks to the driver, she walked off towards the glass-plated entrance to the apartment block leaving Giancarlo to tip the driver before following on behind.

The concierge was at his station, watching his portable TV set which sat beside his security monitor. He glanced up and smiled in recognition as he pressed the button to release the door lock. By the time the doors went swinging open Giancarlo was beside her and, with the usual exchange of polite good evenings with the concierge, they were making their way over to the lift.

As it took them upwards Natalia found herself making a comparison with this journey and the last one they had made together like this. Last time he had been crowding her into the corner, pulsing with suppressed emotion and ready for a different kind of showdown. Now they stood about as far apart as two people could get in such a confined space.

The lift stopped, the doors opened, she walked into the white-tiled private foyer, hesitated only for a moment before walking on again, passing the opening to the office on her left because she was no longer interested in doing that kind of business with this man. She walked by the sitting-room entrance because she'd never liked that room and if there was going to have to be a showdown then she wasn't putting herself so close to the bedroom when it happened. Which left only the dining room she liked about as much as the sitting room, and the kitchen, which was about the only place left.

Walking in, she went directly to the fridge and got herself a small bottle of sparkling water and a glass, then went to sit down at the table. She was just removing the plastic cap when Giancarlo strode in. Almost ghosting her actions, he went to the fridge to get himself a can of cola instead of water.

The tab went fizz. Her water hissed as it hit the glass. He walked over to stand staring out of the darkened window while she sat staring down at her glass. His arm lifted as he took a drink from his can. She took a sip of the sparkling water. Other than for those two relatively innocent actions nothing else stirred in the room if you didn't include the roaring speed with which two like-minded brains were working.

He began the battle. 'Will you marry me, Natalia?' he asked...

No answer, he noted. Did you really expect one? he then wryly asked himself. Only to wince when she suddenly started laughing, not loudly or hysterically but disdainfully.

'You've got a nerve,' she said.

Oh, I don't know, he silently countered, staring grimly down at his can. It is a lack of nerve that made me ask the question. I am in dire straits here or the shrewd gambler in me would not be putting my last card on the table first.

'You can't even bring yourself to ask me that to my face,' she added scathingly.

The jeer spun him round to face her. She was sitting there glaring an evil spell at him like the beautiful blue-eyed witch he always saw, and on a grunt of rueful surrender he threw himself in at the deep end.

'I fell in love with you at first glance across a packed company dining room,' he informed her. 'Is that in your face enough for you?'

He could see that it most definitely was not. She had turned white again, very white, and the eyes had gone grey, permeating the air with a frost of cold disbelief. 'You fell in *lust* with me, you mean,' she denounced in disgust.

'That too,' he agreed, adding a wry shrug because it was the truth, and he was determined that they would only deal with the truth from here on in. 'But at the time I believed you were my brother-in-law's mistress and the woman who was threatening to ruin his marriage.'

'Oh, that makes it all okay, then,' she mocked him bitterly.

'What else was I supposed to think?' He sighed out impatiently. 'Have you any idea what such a belief did to me?'

'I know what it did to you!' she threw back angrily. 'It turned you into a rat, and a deceiver!'

'That's great,' he derided. 'Coming from the woman who has been lying to me from day one.'

'At least I lied to protect someone I loved.'

'So did I,' he reminded her. 'Alegra is just as important to me as Edward is to you.'

'Only your way of protecting those you love was deliberately geared towards a bit of good old-fashioned Sicilian revenge at the same time,' she pointed out. 'My *reasons* for being with you were honest, Giancarlo. Whereas yours were only ever intended to cause me pain.'

He said nothing. The silence hung like a cloud between them because there really was no answer to her last bitter claim. So on a heavy sigh he changed tack, by ridding himself of his can and coming to pull out the chair beside her. Swinging it around, he then straddled it and sat down while she watched all of this with a distinctly wary look in her eye.

That was okay, he told himself. He could deal with wary better than he could deal with bitterness and pain. So he folded his arms along the chair back, placed his chin on the top of them, and, with her gaze held captive by her own wariness of what was coming, he repeated gently:

'Marry me,' and he smiled...

The smile hit dead centre, the proposal sent her head dizzy. And his wretched eyes were warming her right through! It was like being in the company of the world's most accomplished beguiler! It just wasn't fair—none of it! Did he honestly think she didn't know what he was trying to do?

'Listen to me,' she said, having to push the words up through a thickened throat because, really, she had no defence worth mentioning against this man, and she was beginning to weaken, she could feel it happening. 'Let's get a few things straight before this gets entirely out of hand,' she suggested. 'In the unlikely event that I am pregnant, I do not expect or even want an offer of marriage from you. It is neither necessary nor expected in this day and age. And I've been there,' she reminded him. 'I know what it's like to be a child of a single parent. There's no stigma in that label any more. If or when I need to do so, I will cope as my mother coped. I don't even mind!' she added in the hope that it would be of some help to him. 'So don't cut yourself up thinking you have to offer marriage to Edward's bastard daughter because you made a few mistakes about her. Especially when we both know we were never so much as heading in that direction before tonight's—mess came to light. What we had here was never very real, but just a window in time we both used to enjoy each other. But tomorrow or next week or—whenever, you can go back to Milan or Sicily or—wherever, and that window will close, as it should do. So don't try to keep it open out of some misguided sense of honour you feel you need to redress,' she begged. 'Nothing in this life is absolutely certain. We all make mistakes, change, move on. Let's not further clutter up the baggage we take with us, with a set of marriage vows neither of us wanted to make in the first place!'

To give him his due, he listened. He listened without comment and without expression as she rambled through her wise little speech. His forearms remained folded across the chair back, his eyes didn't move from her beautiful face. When she finally fell into an empty little silence, he simply allowed a small pause to hover after it, then repeated quietly:

'Marry me...'

Natalia erupted out of nowhere. 'Oh, stop it!' she cried, wondering just what it took to get through to this man! 'Why are you doing this? You know it isn't what you really want!'

'You don't *know* what I want,' he shot right back. 'Try asking me instead of telling me!'

'No,' she refused, because she felt she had already covered it as far as she was concerned.

She went to get up. His hand closing around her wrist stopped her. Electricity sizzled along her veins and she felt a wild rush of sheer excitement. Angrily she pulled free.

She had to get out of here, she decided urgently, before he really started getting to her! And she jumped to her feet, then immediately wished she hadn't done that when old dizziness dropped over her.

Seeing it happen, Giancarlo uttered a choice curse as he leapt up himself, then was impatiently kicking his chair aside so he could pull her against him. 'Don't go faint on me again,' he commanded harshly. 'This is no time for passing out. We need to deal with this!'

'I thought I was dealing with it!' she snapped, feeling so light-headed that she had to lean against him.

'No, you were talking utter rubbish,' he arrogantly opined. 'I just let you get it off your chest because you seemed to need to.'

Well, thanks, she thought grimly. 'Let me go, please.'

Instead he bent to hook his arm beneath her knees and the next thing she knew she was being cradled against his chest and he was striding out of the kitchen and down the hallway to the only room she expected him to take her to.

The bedroom. The bed, where he settled her down on the top of the covers then came to lie beside her. 'Sex isn't the way to solve this particular problem,' she drawled in acid derision.

'Sex isn't what I'm after,' he said, coming up on one elbow so he could look directly into her angry blue eyes. 'I simply wanted you safely horizontal just in case you decided to do something else stupid.'

I'm stupid. I talk rubbish, Natalia grimly listed. I can't be relied upon to take care of my own safety. And, he no longer wants sex from me.

'Now,' he said firmly. 'Ask me.'

'Ask you what?' she flashed, wishing she didn't just love having him this close to her.

'What I want from this relationship,' he provided, bringing the whole darn thing back to the last place she wanted it.

Oh, play the game and get it over with! she told herself frantically because he was too close and she was beginning to feel... 'What is it you want from this relationship, Giancarlo?' she enquired very wearily.

His eyes went black. It was like looking into some terrible place where her fate lay waiting. 'You,' he murmured huskily. 'I want you. I adore you. You are my life. So—will you marry me?'

'You're crazy,' she breathed, closing her eyes on a sigh of burning frustration. 'You just don't listen.' The eyes flew back open. 'You didn't even know who I really was until a couple of hours ago! So how can you know you want to marry this person?'

'Because she is the mother of my child,' he answered smoothly.

'I might not be pregnant!' she reminded him. 'Aren't you jumping the gun a bit?'

'That is not the point.' He smiled that electrifying smile again. 'In believing you could be pregnant, I discovered how much I loved the idea. So the rest does not really matter. You are the woman I want as the mother of my children. So—will you marry me?'

It was easier to close her eyes again and pretend he just wasn't there, she decided. A stupid idea when the man was lying right here beside her on a bed they had been sharing for weeks now, she mocked her own idiocy.

And to further mock the whole thing, his hand came up to brush a feather-light finger across the arch of her eyelashes where they lay flickering against her cheeks. 'I will cherish and adore you all of your life,' he promised huskily.

'Last week you were still plotting my ruin,' she replied.

He touched his lips to her stubborn mouth. 'I loved you even when I was plotting your ruin. Does that not count for anything?' he asked, moving on to nibble at one of her earlobes.

She had to move her shoulder in an effort to dislodge him—or start quivering. 'Is this the Sicilian way of being diplomatic?' she asked. 'If so, I have to tell you it doesn't work very well.'

He just laughed softly in his throat, which brought on the quiver anyway. 'I loved you even when I knew you were lying through your lovely white teeth to me,' he pointed out. 'Like the cool-headed denial you gave about not knowing the combination to Edward's safe, for instance...'

Her eyes flicked open. 'How do you know that I knew it?' she demanded.

His eyes were taunting, like his voice when he said, 'Because I listened in to the message Edward had left you on your voice-mail.'

'Is that why you asked me for the combination?' she gasped. 'Just to see what I would say?'

He nodded. 'It is also the reason why you have been working from here ever since,' he added. 'When you wouldn't give up the combination I decided I had to get you away from the safe. So I set up this place.' He glanced around them. 'So quickly you won't believe how much trouble I took.'

'But why?' she cried. 'Why should my father's private papers be so important to you?'

'Ah,' he drawled. 'But you are thinking like a daughter instead of a mistress,' he pointed out. 'I saw whatever was in that safe as your—payment let's say, for services rendered. And I enjoyed very much making sure you couldn't get your sticky hands on that payment.'

'Money, you mean,' she realised angrily. 'How cynical a mind do you actually have, Giancarlo?'

'Worse than you think,' he freely admitted. 'I had the safe opened by a locksmith the day after you came here to work. I found nothing inside it but Edward's private stock portfolio. And since I put that together for him, I presumed that whatever it was he didn't want me to see had already been taken—by his lovely accomplice—along with a genuine Fabergé watch, for instance.'

'You believed I'd actually stolen my great-grandmother's watch?' Natalia just stared at him, stunned by the depths his mind had her wallowing! 'Edward kept details of my birth in there,' she explained because she could see no reason not to now. 'I managed to get them out before you arrived in the next morning.' She now felt rather pleased with herself for doing that. 'Though I did so because Edward was so sure you had the safe combination somewhere—not because I expected you to resort to using a locksmith to get into it!'

'Machiavellian, that's me.' He smiled. 'You know I had mislaid the piece of paper he had written the combination on, so I had to resort to other methods.'

'Nothing is too low for you, is it?' she breathed.

'Will you still marry me knowing that?'

'I never said I was ever going to marry you,' she pointed out.

His answer was to swoop on her mouth. It just wasn't fair, Natalia complained helplessly. He was applying unfair tactics and she couldn't resist him and the fact that he knew that only made it all the more unfair!

'You said no sex,' she mumbled against his mouth.

'This is not sex,' he denied, moving his lips to her cheek then back to let them hover a hair's breadth away from hers again. 'It is showing my adoration for the woman who belongs to me.'

And to give his claim substance he began gently rotating the hand he had lying against her abdomen. Silk began to move sensually against her skin, the heat from his hand making it all the more pleasurable. She liked it, and didn't want to like it. And worst of all, his eyes were so dark and warm and incredibly tender that she felt herself starting to sink into them.

'Marry me,' he urged with husky softness. 'Let me be your husband, your lover and your devoted soul mate.'

'You're just hedging your bets in case I am pregnant,' she derided, but she made sure her lips made fleeting contact with his as she spoke. 'Come tomorrow when you find I am not, you'll be straining at the leash to escape.'

'Our child is growing in here,' he murmured softly. 'Just think of it. Or think of all the passionate nights we will have trying to put the seed there if it has not made it already.' And to punctuate his point his hand began to slowly ruche up her dress. She gasped in response; he rewarded the revealing little sound with another kiss.

'So, marry me,' he repeated.

'I can't marry you,' she breathed. 'I know you're only offering it because you feel some misguided need to redress an error.'

'Or because you don't love me...?' he softly suggested.

'Oh,' she choked, and brought up her fingers to place them against his mouth. 'Stop it,' she pleaded.

His eyes went so black she thought she could see right inside him, down as far as his pulsing heart. And he kissed the fingers, then reached up to remove them. 'Marry me,' he repeated.

Could she do it? she asked her weaker side. Could she dare to marry this man who had used her so appallingly...?

She was wavering; Giancarlo could feel her need to give in to him throbbing beneath his caressing hand.

'Marry me,' he said again, and felt that throbbing beat of desire pulse through him like an extra heartbeat.

She was his, he could feel it. The warmth of her lips told him, the tremor of her body. All she needed to do was whisper *yes* and the rest would take care of itself for now. 'What can be so wrong in marrying this man who wants you so badly, hmm? Marry me, *amore*,' he urged yet again, 'and I will promise to love you for ever.'

Love, the keyword, he noted as her blue eyes turned warm and dark and sultry. 'Yes,' she whispered.

Triumph filled his head, followed almost immediately by a different sensation entirely that lost them both the will to think at all for the next few exquisite minutes while he paid homage to that tiny 'yes'.

Then the telephone began to ring, bringing them both screeching back to reality with a jolt. He lifted his head, frowning in irritation because it was gone three in the morning and who the hell rang anyone at—?

'Edward,' Natalia said jerkily, and was trying to stretch over him to pick up the phone even as he snatched it up.

His arm wrapped around her, keeping her close. 'Yes?' he prompted, Natalia's fear becoming his fear when he heard his sister's voice coming back at him.

'Edward will not settle down and rest because he's worrying about his daughter,' Alegra snapped at him with failing patience with the man she loved. 'If Natalia is with you will you please put her on this telephone so she can reassure her father that you are not seducing her—again!'

'But I am seducing her,' Giancarlo drawled lazily, settling back onto the pillows and taking Natalia with him. 'You interrupted us, in fact,' he added, then coolly held the receiver to Natalia's ear so she could receive the full blast of his sister's anger instead of him.

From being white-faced with fear she was suddenly blushing. He began to grin, all wicked white teeth and Italian devilry. 'He—he isn't bullying me,' she replied to whatever Alegra had said. 'We were—talking,' she tagged on not very convincingly. Then— 'Edward!' she sighed out. 'Will you listen to me?'

Edward? The grin altered to a frown and he snatched the phone back from her ear. 'Edward,' he said, cutting the older man off mid angry flood. 'I would formally like to ask for the hand of your daughter in marriage.'

'No!' Natalia choked. 'Don't tell him that!'

'Yes, of course she has accepted me. Do you honestly think I am going to allow her to look elsewhere now?'

At which point Natalia sank back against the pillow and closed her eyes in an act of surrender. Seeing it happen, Giancarlo smiled to himself, and settled back to convince his angry brother-in-law that the woman in his arms was going to be so cherished that her papa had no need at all to worry.

'Okay?' he questioned when eventually he was allowed to replace the receiver.

'No,' Natalia replied. 'I feel like a hostile takeover. No trick too mean, no bribe too low. He did give you his blessing, I am presuming?'

'With the promise that he will be well enough to give you away at our wedding next week.'

'Next week,' she repeated as his arms looped round her and he pulled her into the crook of his body.

'You smell of woman,' he growled, nuzzling her earlobe.

'You said no sex.'

'I changed my mind.'

'What if I decide to change my mind about marrying you?'

'Too late,' he murmured, moving on to nibble at the corner of her mouth. 'We are officially betrothed in the eyes of my family. Pull out now and they will feel honour bound to avenge my broken heart.'

'You Sicilians have life all neatly packaged whichever way you want to look at it, don't you?'

'It is in the genes,' he explained, while stringing soft, light kisses across her full bottom lip now. 'We are very serious about family honour.'

Serious about other things, too, she thought as her body arched in response to what his hands were doing to her. 'And if I am *not* pregnant?' she asked on a last-gasp attempt to make sure everything was clear between them on this point.

'I will *make* you pregnant,' he declared, then set about showing her exactly how he intended to go about it...

The next morning she was sitting at the kitchen table drinking juice when he wandered in from the office. 'Well?' he said.

'No,' Natalia quietly replied. 'The test was negative.'

Giancarlo went still for a moment to take this in, while she sat there staring fixedly at her drink and hoping to goodness that he wouldn't see how frightened she was that this negative response was going to change everything.

Then a pair of hands came around her waist. Warm hands, strong hands, exquisitely familiar hands that firmly propelled her out of her chair, then guided her into the circle of his arms.

'Will you marry me, Natalia?' he softly proposed to her.

She looked up warily, wondering if this was some kind

of joke. 'You've asked me that question a million times already,' she mocked him.

'And you said yes, once, under duress. So now I ask it again. Will you marry me because you want to do so more than anything else? Will you marry me because I want you to do so more than anything else? And will you marry me because I love you more than anyone else?'

Her heart began to swell. Tears flooded her eyes. 'Yes,' she whispered. 'Because I love you more than anything else.'

'There.' He smiled. 'Now we both understand each other. It feels good, hmm?'

Oh, yes, she thought as she folded her arms tightly around him. It feels very good…

EPILOGUE

STANDING here on what felt like the edge of the world, Natalia gazed out on the silver-tipped navy-blue waters of a moon-kissed ocean, and wondered if a single day could ever be more perfect than this one had been.

Down there just beneath her she could see her father and Alegra strolling hand in hand along one of the many pathways that threaded through the terraced garden. Every so often they would stop and their two heads would come together over the tiny bundle Alegra held safely cradled in the crook of her arm.

Our son, Natalia thought tenderly, and felt her heart swell in her breast with the love Alessandro brought into all their lives. His arrival two months ago had been a blessing in so many ways. For her father and Alegra, Alessandro had been the final ingredient they'd needed to help heal old wounds and replace their grief for their lost son with a newfound joy who apparently looked so much like their beloved Marco.

If you didn't count the eyes, Natalia thought smilingly. For Alessandro's eyes were most definitely like her own eyes—as Giancarlo never ceased to complain. 'How am I supposed to be the strong father when he only has to look at me and I melt?' he liked to say to defend what a soft touch he was where his son was concerned.

He too had undergone a dramatic healing, she acknowledged, thinking back to the day she had tentatively suggested to him that his son should be christened in Sicily. She'd expected a knock-back—had even been prepared for it with all her reasons at the ready to fiercely argue the point with him. But after only a few short moments of sober contemplation, Giancarlo had lifted his dark head to look at her, and it had all been there. The need, the hunger to see his homeland again, the readiness to heal that final part of him by taking happiness back to the place where only pain and grief had been left behind.

So here they were, all five of them fresh from a beautiful christening service in the same beautiful little church Giancarlo himself had once been christened in, followed up by a celebratory dinner shared in this beautiful place perched high on a Sicilian hillside, which overlooked a small piece of heaven.

She sighed happily.

'What was that for?' a deep voice enquired behind her.

'Come and look,' she urged, and felt a pair of familiar hands slide around her waist as Giancarlo joined her at the open window. As usual her bones melted at his closeness and she sank back against him. His chin came to rest on the top of her head and her hands drifted up to link fingers with his where they lay across her stomach. 'Do you see what I see?' she asked him.

'And what do you see?' he prompted.

'I see a beautiful night in a beautiful place, with two beautiful people and a beautiful child,' she softly confided. 'It was the right thing to do, wasn't it?' she then questioned anxiously. 'You all do feel much better for coming back here?'

His mouth brushed a kiss to the top of her head. 'Marco is no longer a ghost that haunts us, but a loving memory we have learned to cherish,' he quietly confirmed.

'Good,' she said, and sighed again in absolute contentment. 'Then everything is truly perfect.'

'Ah, you were wanting true perfection?' Giancarlo drawled.

His tone alone had her senses quickening, the soft feeling of contentment fleeing in the face of something much more elemental that was suddenly sizzling in the air.

'No, Giancarlo,' she firmly denied it. 'We can't make love now. Alessandro—'

'Is in the safest hands I know besides our own,' he inserted, then was reaching out to pull shut the bedroom window, before turning her to face him.

His eyes were gleaming with sensual promises; her body began to pulse in response. He bent down to kiss her, she sighed and let him because—when had she ever been able to resist this man? His fingers found the zip to her dress, and she quivered as it drifted down her spine.

'You really are incorrigible sometimes,' she informed him ruefully.

'You wanted perfection,' he countered innocently. 'I am the man who is so in love with you that he constantly strives to give you everything your beautiful heart desires.'

'I thought I *had* perfection,' Natalia dryly pointed out.

'No,' he denied. '*This* is perfection, *mia cara*...'

He was right and it was.

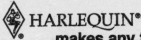

*Harlequin truly does
make any time special....
This year we are celebrating
weddings in style!*

A Walk Down the Aisle
WEDDING CELEBRATION

To help us celebrate, we want you to tell us how wearing the Harlequin wedding gown will make your wedding day special. As the grand prize, Harlequin will offer one lucky bride the chance to **"Walk Down the Aisle" in the Harlequin wedding gown!**

There's more...

For her honeymoon, she and her groom will spend five nights at the **Hyatt Regency Maui.** As part of this five-night honeymoon at the hotel renowned for its romantic attractions, the couple will enjoy a candlelit dinner for two in Swan Court, a sunset sail on the hotel's catamaran, and duet spa treatments.

A HYATT RESORT AND SPA

MAUI
the Magic Isles

Maui • Molokai • Lanai

To enter, please write, in, 250 words or less, how wearing the Harlequin wedding gown will make your wedding day special. The entry will be judged based on its emotionally compelling nature, its originality and creativity, and its sincerity. This contest is open to Canadian and U.S. residents only and to those who are 18 years of age and older. There is no purchase necessary to enter. Void where prohibited. See further contest rules attached. Please send your entry to:

Walk Down the Aisle Contest

In Canada	In U.S.A.
P.O. Box 637	P.O. Box 9076
Fort Erie, Ontario	3010 Walden Ave.
L2A 5X3	Buffalo, NY 14269-9076

You can also enter by visiting www.eHarlequin.com
Win the Harlequin wedding gown and the vacation of a lifetime!
The deadline for entries is October 1, 2001.

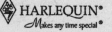

HARLEQUIN®
Makes any time special ®

PHWDACONT1